JUST A LITTLE AUTOMATIC WEAPONS FIRE IN YOUR LOCAL NUCLEAR POWER PLANT . . .

MONSTER MELT-DOWN

"Jess, tell them to do a shutdown!"

They can't. The main computer is crashed and the monsters have control of the manual overrides.

"Then tell them to get clear!" Scampering down the stairs, I kicked open a locked wire-mesh door, and ducked as a ricochet went past my head. Shotgun in one hand, flamethrower in the other, Father Donaher gave suppressing cover. Ten meters across, the were-wolves were wildly spraying us with small caliber bullets. George cut loose with the Masterson Assault Cannon. Their bodies jerking wildly, the wolves did a little dance of death as the high-explosive and now silver-tipped mini-shells blew them to hell. Jessica did mop-up with the Uzi.

But then the largest werewolf pulled a small velvet bag from his flak jacket and tossed it at us. Expanding, the bag tore apart as out stepped one mother-ugly monster. A weresquid. Silver meant bupkis to this thing. I placed my last four shots into the pulsating chest of the wiggling wonder. It didn't even notice.

And then the sirens started to howl . . .

FULL MOONSTER

NICK POLLOTTA

ACE BOOKS, NEW YORK

This novel is based upon the role-playing game, BUREAU 13 STALKING THE NIGHT FANTASTIC, by TriTac Systems, P.O. Box 61, Madison Heights, MI 48071. Copyright © 1982. Used with the permission of Richard Tucholka, owner, creator, and president.

This book is an Ace original edition,
and has never been previously published.

FULL MOONSTER

An Ace Book / published by arrangement with
the author

PRINTING HISTORY
Ace edition / August 1992

ISBN: 0-441-08421-4

10   9   8   7   6   5   4   3   2   1

With fond memories and warmest regards to the Philadelphia Science Fiction Society, and the Sunday afternoon gang of crazies at Chestnut Hall: Oz Fontecchio, Barbara Higgins, Luke Thalmeyer, Frank Richards, JoAnne Lawler, Larry Gelfand, Joyce Carrol, John Prentis, T-Burn, John and Laura Symms, and especially to the vivacious Debbie Malamut.

Okay, who brought the pizza?

FULL MOONSTER

INITIATION

Prologue

The scream came from out of nowhere.

Splitting the forest night like an endless explosion, the raw-throated cry of anguish wavered and wassailed until it abruptly ended in a meaty thump. In perfect harmony, the mountain cabin shook; pictures and diplomas went lopsided, mugs danced off bookshelves and the glass door of a surgical instrument cabinet cracked.

Rising from her easy chair by the fireplace, Dr. Joanne Abernathy threw aside the medical journal and hobbled over to a window. Dear God, what was that horrible noise? Had somebody fallen off Deadman's Cliff?

Drawing back the lace curtains, the panels of thermal tempered glass segmented her view of the Canadian forest into tiny squares. Pressing her nose flat against the pane, the veterinarian frantically peered out. Illuminated by the full moon overhead, the trees were frosted by the silver light making green seem black and black turn invisible. Completely filling the northern horizon was the ragged gray expanse of the MacKenzie palisades: an irregular series of sheer angular foothills that bisected this isolated area of the Yukon wilderness like an insane granite wall.

Then the howl sounded again, closer this time, and faintly overhead could be heard a jetliner streaking off into the distance. An odd thought came to Abernathy, who promptly dismissed it. Anybody falling out of a plane would be dead from cranial blood loss before hitting the ground. And afterwards? Well, you'd simply fill in the impact crater with a bulldozer and put a tombstone any ol' damn place that seemed proper.

But if some poor bastard had accidently tumbled off the cliff . . .

Hurriedly, the retired vet retrieved her teeth from a glass of water set on the stone hearth, pulled on her walking shoes and grabbed a flashlight. After forty years of birthing calves, inoculating sheep and fixing broken bones for both man and beast, there was little she couldn't patch. If the luckless sonofabitch was still alive when she got there, he or she had a good chance of staying that way. And as the closest thing to a doctor in these parts, Abernathy was duty bound to heal even incompetent hunters who tumbled off mountains. Darn fool was probably drunk.

Pulling on a light cloth coat, the woman paused for a moment at the gun rack. This wasn't downtown Whitehead. There were pumas and grizzly in this area, neither of which gave a hoot about her Hellenic oath, but only how tasty old folk were. Bypassing the big-bore 30.06 Winchester as too cumbersome to use with her arthritis, she started to take the Browning .22 carbine, but then decided no. It was only a varmint rifle and so incredibly lightweight that it floated if dropped in water. Obviously, a compromise was the answer.

Yanking open the hall closet, she retrieved a bulky leather belt from a peg on the wall. Dutifully, the vet strapped it about her waist and checked the load in the shiny clean Webley .44 revolver. She had never fired the weapon except in practice sessions and once, only once, to put a rabid opossum out of its misery. Afterwards she had burned the corpse and gotten very drunk.

Unbolting the front door, the woman clicked on the porch lights and stepped outside. The forest was strangely quiet. Weird. Testing the wind with a damp finger, she guesstimated that the noise had come from the direction of the old salt lick and started east. After a few dozen meters the trail angled off in another direction, so Abernathy took advantage of a fresh bear tunnel to continue towards the cliff. She moved fast and silent along the collapsed line of bushes that marked the regular passage of a large bear. A griz, perhaps. Thankfully, the droppings smelled old.

Minutes later, she found the moaning creature buried under a pile of leaves by a copse of tall evergreen trees. The white beam of her flashlight displayed little of the animal besides its hind legs, but those were enough. Joanne knew a wolf when she saw one. This, however, was the biggest she had ever seen. The paws were large as a grown man's foot. Enormous!

Laying her flashlight on the rocky ground to shine on the wolf, the vet gently brushed aside the leaves and uncovered the wounded animal. The beast whimpered at the intrusion, but offered no resistance. Black blood was matted heavy on the chest and there was a reddish foam about its snout. Joanne frowned. Damn. Possible internal bleeding. There wasn't much she could do for that here. Glancing upward, she was not surprised to see a leafy hole through the tree branches overhead. The ground here was a flat outcropping of stone, torn branches and smashed bushes forming a natural cushion under the dying wolf. The angle was wrong, but the creature must have fallen off the cliff. What else made sense?

Keeping well clear of the dagger-sharp teeth, Abernathy examined the beast closer. The wolf was shivering and panting, but its nose was bone dry. Trained fingers checked its ears and eased back an eyelid. Damnation, the pulse rate was down, and the temperature was up. The wolf seemed to be suffering from more than mere impact damage. Suspicious, the vet turned her flashlight directly on the bloody chest and got an answer. Yep, gunshot. But the wound in the chest was only superficial, made by a .22, or .32 at the most. Ye god, were the frigging poachers using poisoned bullets again? Anything to save the pelt from additional damage. Damn them. There was a difference between hunting for food and killing for fashion. Morally, ethically and legally.

Furious, Abernathy hoped that the slug hadn't hit any bones so the ballistics lab of the Royal Mounties could get a good reading off the round. With any luck they would be able to track the poacher by the identifying marking from his/her rifle and slam the stupid sonofabitch into jail. Wolves were an endangered species, protected by international law!

On the other hand, if there were massive internal injuries compounded by poisoning, there might be nothing she could do to help. Tentatively, Joanne drew the Webley .44. Unexpectedly, the beast extended a shaking paw to gently touch the gun barrel and push it away in an amazingly human gesture.

In ragged stages, Abernathy reholstered the handgun and knelt alongside the wolf to tenderly stroke its head. A hot tongue licked at her wrist.

"Okay, *loup*," she softly crooned. "No mercy killing. I'd rather not anyway. Somehow, I'll get you back to the cabin and fix you proper. *Nous, mon ami?*"

But there was no response. The wolf had fallen unconscious.

Realizing that time was now against her, the elderly vet moved fast. Placing her pocket handkerchief on the oozing wound, she cinched her belt tight about the chest. The wolf stirred and mewed in pain, but did not lash out with its deadly paws and the bleeding slowed.

Next, using her belt knife, the woman split some of the fallen tree limbs and crisscrossed the branches through the sleeves of her coat to jury-rig a drag. Gently, she rolled the huge animal onto the makeshift litter and the limp wolf actually seemed to assist in the task. This was either a hell of an intelligent animal or else somebody's escaped pet.

Buttoning the coat closed to keep the wolf in place, Abernathy grabbed the pockets of the garment and began the arduous task of dragging the wounded beast through the woods. An hour of backbreaking labor later, vet and patient were at the cabin. Gasping, the elderly woman thanked God for the new bear tunnel or else she never would have made it here. The colossal animal must weigh a hundred kilos! Almost as much as a full-grown man. Maybe more.

The shed at the rear of the cabin was on ground level, easy to get into, but unheated. So the oldster nearly busted a gut hauling the hairy giant up the inclined wooden ramp used for conveying fireplace logs into the house.

As she closed the front door, Joanne took a moment to catch her breath. Getting the poor thing onto the dining table was out of the question. The surgery would have to be done here in the living room. It would be messy, but the battered rug had seen worse. Her monthly poker game with the local Eskimo tribe always added a few more beer and bloody-nose stains to the old Sears two-ply anyway. Someday, she really would have to give the rug a serious cleaning. Or just burn it and buy a new one.

Retrieving her medical bag from the hall closet, Joanne loaded a glass hypodermic needle with a clear liquid, tapped out the air bubble and injected the moaning animal with 10cc of morphine. Audibly, the beast sighed in relief as the pain diminished. She followed with a wide-spectrum antibiotic. The bacteriological compound was an inexpensive sulfur mixture, the only type she could afford. It wasn't as powerful as the new crystal silver formulas, but it didn't require refrigeration after mixing and would do the job. Wisely, she decided that the distemper and rabies vaccine could wait till later. Step one: get that bullet out.

In the kitchen, Joanne threw an assortment of instruments into a sterilization steamer and washed her hands. Returning to the living room, she switched on every light in the place. Grabbing a jack-and-shackle arrangement from the top of a bookcase, Abernathy knelt to tie the animal's forelegs to a plastic support. Carefully, she extended the framework to separate the legs and expose the chest for ease of accessibility, then removed the belt and handkerchief and washed the chest wound clean with an astringent solution and white cotton cloth. The animal moaned weakly and she touched the big vein in a stiff ear. Pulse rate was low but steady. She had bought some time. She hoped it would be enough. Rummaging in her medical bag, Joanne found what she wanted and used electric clippers to shave the area around the entry wound bare. Next, the vet packed the opening with #4 surgical sponges, finishing just in time for the sterilizer to ding.

She raced back to the kitchen, where she used pot holders to handle the hot instruments, then returned to the living room and laid them down on a pristine rectangle of white cloth. Taking a slim steel rod in hand, Joanne spoke softly to the delirious animal as she began to probe for the bullet.

Abernathy knew that wild animals responded to words and could feel your true intentions better than most people. Many a fur trapper faking friendship found that out the hard way. Wolves were smart.

Surprisingly, the elderly vet located the slug immediately, lodged just under the outer layer of fatty tissue, directly between the main lateral pectoral muscle and the fourth rib. A glancing entry. Thank God.

Extracting the probe, Joanne used long-finger forceps to remove the silvery blob of metal. There came the expected well of blood with its removal, but that soon stopped. Wary of the poisonous coating, she placed the slug on a cotton gauze pad and then into a plastic specimen bottle, which she dropped into a pocket. There. The Mounties would want to see that. Odd, though. The bullet didn't appear to be coated with anything. And the metal was surprisingly soft. Definitely not steel or cold iron. It resembled silver. That gave her pause. Somebody had shot a wolf with a silver bullet?

The breathing of the wolf increased and it moaned softly.

Shaking the wild thoughts from her mind, Joanne pivoted to gather needle and thread from her medical bag. But when she turned to suture the wound, the hole was already closed. Eh? Dr. Abernathy blinked to clear her eyes of the illusion. Yet the impossible scene stayed the same. The wound had shut by itself. Incredible!

Then as the dumbfounded vet watched, the bullet hole healed completely, without even the slightest puckering or discolorization of the skin to mark its presence. And the hair began to grow with fantastic speed, filling the shaved patch in mere moments.

Horrified, Joanne backed away from the undamaged thing lying sprawled on her rug and retreated to the bedroom. She slammed and locked the door in an automatic response. With shaky knees, the old woman dropped into the bed. Frantically, the veterinarian searched for a scientific explanation of the phenomenon, but none presented itself. Facing the mirror above her dresser, she examined under her eyes, extended a tongue, then checked pulse and temperature. Mentally, she juggled a few algebraic equations, then nodded. Okay, not ill or blatantly senile. Well, then, what had she just witnessed? Magic? Preposterous!

And yet, the folk who lived in the deep woods swapped stories about magical creatures they encountered. Beings who talked, or changed shape, or couldn't be killed: human ghosts, angakok, Indian spirits, the windigo and countless Sasquatch. But to actually encounter a . . . a . . .

Werewolf?

Without conscious thought, Joanne reached into the night table alongside her bed and withdrew a half-full bottle of Alaskan Gold whiskey. She pulled the cork with her teeth, almost losing her dentures in the act, and proceeded to liberally administer a heroic dose of liquid courage to herself.

Just then, something crashed against the locked door and began clawing at the oak planks in a wild frenzy of frustration.

Choking on the blended 90 proof, Joanne dropped the bottle and took refuge behind her chair. *Mon Dieu!* The beast was moving already? How fast did this thing heal? Carefully, she listened to the noises coming from the living room. It didn't sound as if the wolf was smashing furniture randomly. The animal's efforts seemed to be directed against that door. But why? It must smell her and desperately want in. To . . . kill her?

Steadfastly denying that notion, the old woman grew adamant. No. The wolf was only disoriented from the morphine and the operation. The animal could have no wish to actually hurt her. She had saved its life!

Forcing herself calm, Abernathy moved swiftly across the room and stood flat against the wall alongside the trembling door. She had to try reasoning with the creature. Werewolves were half human, so they must be able to think. A pause. Or could they? Which was the dominant half, man or beast? The vet didn't know.

"Hush, it's okay," Joanne said in soothing tones. "There's only me in here. You're in no danger. I'm the person who saved your life. I took out the bullet. Remember? The old lady with the white hair? I found you in the forest and fixed your wound."

Silence.

"Remember? Please, remember!" she implored. "I'm your friend! Friend!"

A strident growl was the only response and the door violently vibrated in the framework as a hundred-plus kilos of muscle slammed against the stout portal.

As Joanne listened, the growls turned to slavering, a noise the vet had heard before in her work. The beast wanted what every patient needed after serious blood loss and an operation. Nourishment.

She relaxed with the thought. Yes, of course. That was it. Hunger could make even the most mild of animals crazy. Well, Dr. Joanne Abernathy had the solution to that minor problem!

However, getting to the kitchen was another matter.

The pounding on the door increased and the hinges started to rattle as Joanne slid the bed in front of the portal, then tipped over her dresser as an additional barricade. Screws popped from the jamb and the door began to sag. Trying to control her panic, Abernathy stood with one hand on the light switch and the other on the latch to the hallway door. Any second now . . .

In an explosion of splinters, the first door collapsed. Joanne cut the lights, threw open the kitchen door, dashed through and locked it behind her.

A moment later that door violently shuddered.

She raced to the freezer and unearthed a fifty-pound slab of sugar-cured moose rump that the vet had won with a royal straight flush. Thank God for wild cards. It was a tight fit into the microwave, but she forced the roast in and turned the dial to high. Precious seconds ticked away as the tremendous haunch of meat was electronically thawed and the werewolf clawed a hole in the kitchen door.

With a musical ding, the microwave won the race.

Yanking out the bloody roast, Abernathy slammed it onto the kitchen table and scooted into the living room, closed the flimsy louvered doors and slid the bolt. Designed more for decoration than protection, these wouldn't stop the beast for very long. But at least the panels hid her from sight.

"There," whispered Joanne breathlessly as she pushed the sofa in front of the doorway. "That moose ought to slack the appetite of anything this side of a lumberjack.

"I hope," the woman added. And if not, she had a whole hickory-smoked hog in the shed that was almost as big as the wolf itself! Odd noises came from the kitchen and she peeked in through a crack of the slats to see.

Standing in the middle of the floor, her patient dominated the appliance-filled room. Towering some seven feet tall, the beast was much more human in its manner and stance than before. Must have disguised itself as a common wolf as a purely defensive measure, she deduced. A monster? Me? Sorry, mate. I'm just a timber wolf. Nudge-nudge, wink-wink.

Padding to the table, the beast picked up the warm red slab of moose and sniffed at it appreciatively. Hesitantly, it gave the morsel an inquisitive lick. An expression of disgust crossed its bestial features and with a snarl he threw the massive roast away. A meaty cannonball, the haunch plowed aside pots and pans to career off the spice rack and smash through the curtained window. In a shower of glass, the moose returned to its natural habitat and disappeared into the night.

Empty hands clutching at air, Joanne backed from the door, cold terror chilling her bones. No. The wolf didn't want just any food. An old kill held no interest. It wanted fresh meat. Human meat! It wanted her.

Alive.

A massive shadow darkened the louvered doors.

"Bon appétit, loup!" screamed Joanne as she drew the Webley .44 and emptied the handgun at the dimly seen figure. In spite of her anger, the veterinarian aimed high, trying to frighten the creature. Chunks of wood the size of saucers were blasted out of the slats, and the animal on the other side howled in fury.

But as the hopeful woman holstered the revolver, a huge

paw rammed into one of the holes, sharp talons clawing at the aged hardwood as if it were cardboard. When the cavity was large enough, the beast looked directly at the old woman. And it grinned.

Self-preservation overwhelming her natural reticence, Abernathy moved fast to grab the Remington twin-barrel shotgun off the wall rack and, without bothering to see if it was loaded, rammed both of the barrels into the wolf's face and pulled the two triggers.

The double explosion hurtled the man-beast from the ruined door. Blindly, the animal staggered about screaming and clawing at its face. But as the smoke of the discharge cleared, Abernathy saw the werewolf shake its head and the lead pellets scatter outward as if the beast were merely shucking water off fur.

Merde! Desperate, the oldster lowered the shotgun and glanced about the room. Damn few weapons here. Never needed them before. Pistol empty, shotgun same, no time to load the 30.06. Used the dynamite for fishing. Having little choice, the elderly woman ran out the front door. It locked shut behind her.

In the nighttime cold, without even a coat, her choices were even less clear. Escape on foot? Fat chance. Her horse, Tramp, was in the corral. No good. She had never learned to ride without a saddle. The jeep! Keys were on the hearth inside. Damn! Damn! Damn!

The full moon clearly illuminated the yard around her cabin with a silvery blue light and she cursed the orb in acidic French with a few choice phrases learned from a U.S. Marine who had accidentally cut off his hand with a chain saw.

The woodshed!

Frosty ground crunching beneath her shoes, Joanne hurried across the few meters separating the cabin and the shed. Once inside, she swung the single thick door shut and dropped the big locking bar into place. A cord of split wood was neatly stacked along a wall while a few dozen smoked meats hung from the ceiling. The shed was a hundred years old, built to serve as an icehouse in summer and to be a last refuge for settlers to hide in from attacking Indians, British troops and American Old West desperadoes. The walls were mortarless stone a good meter thick and the door was a seamless expanse of solid oak with four bronze hinges. Although werewolves had not been considered in the original design specifications, it would serve. Then again, maybe they had been. How long had these things been around? Since prehistoric times? Which came first, the were or the wolf?

A bellowing roar of rage thundered in the night, closely followed by the sound of screeching metal, and the woman knew the beast was loose.

Praying silently, the vet backed into a corner pushing her way through the dangling assortment of salt haunches, homemade sausage and dried birds. She took a position by Big Boy, her prize dead hog. Wolves had great vision, but they tracked by scent. With any luck, lost amidst the dozens of smoked meats, her bodily odors would be masked.

Even through the thick stone walls, Abernathy could faintly discern the destruction of her jeep and the screaming death of Tramp. A tear welled in her eye and she used a sleeve. Unable to find her, the wolf was going on a rampage of destruction. Oh God, what had she unleashed upon herself? This was a nightmare! It seemed obvious now that the werewolf had fallen from that passing jetliner, and only the granite ledge had stopped it from forming an impact crater in the soil. If not, then the people who shot the beast would still be in pursuit. They had silver bullets! She only had the useless slug. Oh Lord, oh God, what could an old woman with arthritis do against a creature that took a 20,000-foot drop onto solid rock and was merely stunned?

Until tonight, Joanne had never believed any of the wild stories told around the campfires. Monsters? Creatures of the night? Ridiculous! But now the elderly woman desperately racked her memory for any detail to help her in this fight for life.

Ghostly images of movie monsters filled her mind and Abernathy fought to rid herself of the nonsense and concentrate on what she had heard. Werewolves were . . . people cursed by gypsies, or victims bitten by a werewolf. They only appeared during a full moon. Well, the moon was definitely full. Wolfsbane! They couldn't stand wolfsbane! Yes, but what was it? An herb? A root? A long-drawn howl sounded from outside. Unfortunately, the encyclopedia was in the kitchen and that was no longer a proper environment for scholarly pursuits into toxic botany.

Resting her cheek against the cold stone, Joanne let the rich-flavored scent of wood and meat fill her lungs like a healing potion. Abernathy forced herself to concentrate. She wasn't dead yet. Think, Jo, think. Wait a minute, silver killed werewolves! Or was it only silver bullets? Joanne shook her head. Didn't matter. Certainly no silver bullets. And the slug in her pocket was too distorted to be used without being melted and re-formed. Okay, any silver in the house? Silver knives? Goblets? Hell and damnation, this was a Yukon cabin, not the Montreal Hilton!

Suddenly, a throaty laugh came from the door of the shed and Abernathy knew the beast had found her.

The entire cabin shuddered from the impact of something on the other side of the barred portal. The cord of wood toppled over and the hanging meat danced a ghastly jig. In heart-pounding fear, Joanne glanced about the enclosed structure, but there was no place to run or hide. She was trapped. This was it. Tonight was her final day. Here was where she'd die. And that foul beast would be the last thing she saw before death.

And a great calm came upon the elderly woman, similar to the emotionless elation she experienced when performing a delicate operation. So, what would be the final act of Joanne Gertrude Abernathy upon this Earth? Cowering submission? Hysterics? Suicide?

Several minutes later, the oak beam barring the door finally cracked and the wolf stooped over to enter the shed. Appended on a length of chain, the hundred kilos of hickory-smoked, sugar-cured Big Boy slammed the beast in the face. Roaring in annoyance, the werewolf ripped the giant hog off the steel support hook and tossed the carcass into the litter-filled yard. In the background, the cabin was on fire.

The dancing flames cast eerie shadows inside the darkened shed, but the wolf could still clearly see the old woman standing brazen. She held a machine thing in her hands.

"Okay, *loup*, you want me?" snarled Dr. Abernathy. "Then come and get me!"

The bold defiance puzzled the man-beast for a second, but as the elderly female did not hold the booming-device-which-killed, the wolf steadily advanced.

Yanking on the starter cord, Joanne got the chain saw to come to deadly life. In a stuttering roar, the linked array of carbide-steel teeth moved in a thundering blur of speed.

Brushing aside the brandished log-cutter, the wolf racked a paw at the woman's throat, but Abernathy raised an arm to block. The claws shredded cloth and flesh. The machine fell to the floor. Writhing in agony, Joanne sprawled on her back, trembling fingers trying to staunch the flow of blood from her slashed forearm.

Drooling, the beast came closer.

. . . and from underneath her, Joanne swung the small hand axe used to split kindling. The attack was so pitiful, the werewolf paused in astonishment. And it was only for a single moment that he saw the tiny silver slug neatly impaled on the edge of the axe blade.

It was an impossible gambit and Abernathy's very last chance for life. A wild gamble on a possible flaw in the gypsy legend. A werewolf could only be killed by a silver bullet, that was stated plain and simple. No ifs, ands or buts.

Yet nowhere did it say the monster had to get *shot*.

Guided by the expert knowledge of a trained veterinarian, the axe blade sank into the chest of the beast, directly between the fifth and sixth ribs, missing the sternum entirely and driving the misshapen silver slug deep into the animal's heart.

The wolf screamed in an amazingly human voice and its eyes rolled into its head until only the whites showed. Dropping to his knees, black blood gushed in horrid amounts and the entire body began to shake.

In reverse motion, the full coat of hair withdrew into bare pink skin. The snout retracted and teeth blunted. The ears moved down the side of the changing skull, talons became fingernails. The Z-style joint of the lower canine legs twisted around to become a single knee. The body shortened, a face formed. And in mere seconds there lay on the floor of the shed a naked dead man with an axe in his chest.

Finished wrapping her plaid shirt around the gash in her arm, Joanne climbed shakily to her feet and glared down at the would-be killer. *Sacré bleu*, it had actually worked. He was dead and that meant she was safe. Safe!

Then the elderly woman frowned. Of course, she had the minor problem of a nude corpse on her hands and a home that resembled Quebec after the riots. But those were minor matters compared to the singular implications of her wound.

Deep as the slash was, the blood was slowing in an unnatural manner. If the legends held true, and they had so far, then a bite from a werewolf made you one as well. But did getting clawed also result in the cursed transformation? Even if you killed the first werewolf? Was it an event chain that could be broken, or a series of isolated events each alone and independent? Dr. Abernathy didn't know. And wouldn't. Not until the next full moon.

Exiting the bloody shed, the exhausted woman stumbled into the yard and sat on Big Boy. The possibilities were endless and frightening. Every month to lose her humanity and become a nonsentient animal. To roam the woods and back alleys of towns searching for helpless people to slaughter. And eat.

Calmly watching her home burn to the ground, Abernathy came to a decision. No. She would not let that happen. She would wrap herself in chains every month. Get drunk. Use illegal narcotics to stupefy herself. Anything! But she would not kill again. Ever.

Facing the starry sky, Joanne made a solemn vow.

Doomed as she was, the retired veterinarian would not rest until she found a cure for this horrifying disease of lycanthropy. And find it she would. Even if Abernathy had to move Heaven and Earth to do so!

Heaven and Earth . . . or Hell.

INFORMATION

CLICK "Good evening and here now the news. President Bush today announ—RETTOPSECRETTOPSECRETTOP SECRETTOPSECRETTOPSECRETTOPSECRETTOPSECRET TOPSECRETTOPSECRETTOPSECRETTOPSECRETTOPSEC RETTOPSECRETTOPSECRETTOPSECRETTOPSECRETTOP SECRETTOPSECRETTOPSECRET

SECURITY LEVEL TEN
RED ALERT
EMERGENCY SITUATION
PRIORITY ONE

ATTENTION ALL BUREAU 13 PERSONNEL:

Yesterday, at 14:43 eastern standard time, there occurred somewhere in the continental United States an unprecedented disturbance in our plane of existence. Momentarily, a rift formed between the ethereal dimension and our own universe, a vibrating portal which released a wild energy burst of staggering proportions. In other words, twelve hours ago somebody set off the magical equivalent of a nuclear bomb.

Every telepath in North America has been rendered unconscious and/or dead from the secondary psionic shock waves. Plus, there's not a single functioning crystal ball remaining from the Panama Canal to the Arctic Circle. Temporarily, the Bureau has been made blind and deaf except for such crude electromagnetic communications as this printed message overriding your local television broadcast. A totally unacceptable situation. Who knows what the hostile supernaturals of our country may be doing in this brief interim of unrestricted freedom? The mind boggles. While our physicians and mages try to resuscitate the comatose telepaths, replacement crystal balls are being flown in from around the world. However, TechServ theorizes that the ethereal radiation has already dropped beneath detectable levels, and since there should be no physical destruction from the blast, it will be extremely difficult for us to find the epicenter of the disturbance. Yet pinpoint it we must. And pronto.

ORDERS: As of this moment, all vacations and sick leaves are hereby canceled. Students have graduated early from our Bangor-Maine Training Academy. Retired and/or dead agents have been recalled to active duty. Every field team and solo agent is directed to fully investigate any unusual occurrence, no matter how minor or seemingly inconsequential, even if it does not blatantly involve the supernatural.

Okay, people. We're dealing with the totally unknown here, even more so than usual, so get moving, stay hard, be alert.

And pray.

Horace Gordon
Division Chief, Bureau 13

TOPSECRETTOPSECRETTOPSECRETTOPSECRETTOPSEC
RETTOPSECRETTOPSECRETTOPSECRETTOPSECRETTOP
SECRETTOPSECRETTOPSECRETTOPSECRETTOPSECRET
TOPSECRETTOPSECRETTOPSECRETTOPSECRETTOP . . .

Slam! "Lucy! I'm home! *Aye caramba!* What have you done to your hair?!"

"Waa . . . !"

ACTIVATION

We headed for death at sixty miles per hour.

Had to. That was the speed limit.

As I checked the loads in both of my .357 Magnums, the world moved silently past the bulletproof windows. Swiftly, our RV maneuvered through the thinning traffic of the West Virginia Highway, its sixteen-cylinder engine oblivious to the mountainous terrain we had to overcome. Each steep hill peaked a valley with sharply declining sides and acute curves banked in serpentine ravines. Just over the edge of the berm was an astonishingly deep canyon filled with white-water rapids, jagged boulders and somber metallic signs saying "Please do not feed the grizzly bears your hand."

Trying to appear casual, I surreptitiously raised the Armorlite window. Just in case we encountered any hairy hitchhikers with no respect for the law.

"Everybody ready?" I asked, angling the thirty-eight-foot van off the main road onto a paved secondary route. As we bumped over potholes and dead raccoons, from the aft passenger section of the hugh RV a ragged chorus answered my question.

"Of course, we're prepared, dear."

"*Banzai*, Ed."

"Rock 'n' roll, chief."

"Anti-no, kemo sabe."

"*Da*, comrade Alvarez."

"Hssss . . ."

Taking a fast peek in the rearview mirror, I could see that my team was relaxed, alert and heavily armed. That last response had been from Amigo, the Gila lizard who traveled with us as a pet/bodyguard. Currently, he was lying on the carpeted floor, sunning his belly and digesting a truly impressive meal of crickets. Only two feet long, with a pebbled hide the color of a rainbow, the softly burping desert reptile didn't appear very impressive. Yet Amigo was more loyal than a dog, faster than a fish, smarter than an elected official and deadlier that a grenade in your shorts. If the tiny lizard ever had to battle a pack of lions, it should be even money on the outcome. Should be, but wasn't. Amigo didn't fight fair.

Satisfied with our status, I returned my attention to the road.

Hadleyville, here we come.

Despite the ominous warning received on our television from the big boss, Horace Gordon himself, my team was still in good spirits. This morning we had neatly neutralized a haunted prison in Pittsburgh, ending a ten-year rampage by an irate spirit as we reenacted the execution of the Evil Dr. Salvatore. But this time, just as my team was about to hang me disguised as the deceased physician, there was a last-minute stay from the governor. The ghost was so overcome with elation that he lost his tenuous hold on this plane of reality and faded away forever. Ha! Child's play. Leaving the execution cell, we blessed the building, dynamited the prison and went for lunch.

It was a pleasant success after our failure in the Yukon last month. A werewolf had escaped us by the unprecedented ploy of jumping out of a jet plane at 40,000 feet. By the time we got the pilot to turn around, decrease altitude and slow enough to parachute after the monster, the beast was already dead and a local vet had disappeared. Almost certainly bitten and now an unwilling enemy of humanity. Poor soul. As one of our very few outright failures, the incident had rankled us. Badly.

On the rear couch of the RV, a redheaded giant finished his prayers with a rumbling *amen*. Removing the purple sash from around his collar, Father Michael Xavier Donaher folded the cloth into a neat bundle and placed it inside a small suitcase with the rest of his priestly paraphernalia: rosary, Bible, scapula and shotgun. As always, the good father was dressed in his usual outfit of black cassock, black pants and track shoes.

"Faith, and what do we know about the history of Hadleyville?" rumbled the big priest in his phony Irish brogue. "Any known ghosts? Local monster legends? Devil cults? Young Republicans Club?"

Placing her 35mm Nikon camera back into the bag between us on the front seat, Jessica pressed a few buttons on the dashboard and cycled up a small computer keyboard and monitor. Booting the on-board system, my wife keyed in the security codes and accessed the West Virginia data file. This state had always been a hotbed of paranormal activity, so while in Wheeling for gas, we used a cellular modem at a pay phone to download the appropriate ASCII file into the van's giga-memory bank from our big InfoNet mainframe located in Chicago.

Ye god, I actually understood that hacker babble! Gotta get out more.

Jessica's slim finger dancing on the keyboard, words began scrolling on the screen. "Established as a municipality in 1774," started Jess. "Was a coal mining town until the vein was exhausted in 1905. Population dropped from twenty thousand to four hundred. Wow. Big bootlegging operation in the 1930s. Town converted to tourism in the 1950s. Built a luxury hotel specifically designed for conventions. They hold about one a month there: plumbers' union, Shriners, Elks, WesCon, which is some kind of science fiction convention—all sorts of stuff."

The screen scrolled some more. "Current mayor is a Eugene Synder, police chief is Steven Kissel. Owner slash manager of the hotel is a Gertrude Wilson. Apparently the three of them pretty much run the place."

"Interesting," remarked Donaher as he slid fresh shells into his Remington shotgun. "Sounds like your typical small town. Isolated, incestuous and innocent."

"Except it ain't there no more," Jess noted.

True enough. We had already been on our way here when the telex came in from the State Police and suddenly our recon mission to Hadleyville was elevated to Full Investigation. When any town stops answering every phone, CB and Ham radios, computer modems, Western Union telegraphs, fax machines, etc., this raises suspicions. But when the event occurs at nigh exactly the same time as a transdimensional rift, bingo! We go in, hard, fast and with guns drawn.

Sitting on the third couch was a pale slim man softly cursing as he struggled to unfold a road map and was making a botch of the job. Nice to know there was something the mage wasn't good at doing. Dressed rather conservatively this morning, Raul Horta was wearing a sleeveless black T-shirt decorated with a starry picture of the Milky Way galaxy marked with a tiny red arrow indicating that "you are here." Neon-blue jogging shorts displayed his incredibly pale legs, and his bony feet sported tan yacht-style moccasins complete with ropes, portholes, anchors and a minuscule steering wheel.

"Only a few more miles to the Hadleyville exit," announced Raul's voice from behind the map. He crossed his legs to the sound of the ocean. "Unless I'm reading this wrong and we're actually in Brazil."

"Okay, how about landmarks?" I requested, heroically trying not to tumble the RV off the inclined road. Geez, hadn't any of the builders heard of that nifty invention called a ruler?

"Landmarks?" The map turned around, sideways, and then went upside down. "Ah! There we are. Make a left past the next runaway-truck crash ramp."

"A major historical landmark," quipped George from underneath a camouflage cap. Uncrossing his arms, the gunner straightened his cloth headgear and sat upright. A proper soldier, Mr. Renault had been trying to catch a nap before a possible battle. Appropriately, our plump killer was wearing mottled green U.S. Army fatigues, complete with high-top black GI boots and web-style gun belt holding a holstered Colt .45 automatic. On the seat next to him was a banjo, which made an unnaturally large depression in the cushion.

"Not true," denied Jessica, loading a clip of tranquilizer

darts into a spare Nikon. Her cameras could shoot in more ways than one. Say cheese or die!

"In West Virginia, a truck crash is just another way of saying that tourists are in town," she finished with a grin.

"Ha. I laugh," replied George sleepily. Lowering the brim of the hat, he started to snore. Politely, Amigo echoed him.

Depositing the Nikon into a cushioned bag full of telephoto lenses, Jessica began loading infrared film into an underwater camera. The love of my life had good balance and fine composition. Took nice pictures too.

"Here comes the Hadleyville exit," said Mindy, continuing to sharpen her long curved sword. As always, our ninja was sensibly dressed in combat sneakers and a muted gray jogging suit.

I squinted at the roadway. "What? Where?"

Stroke. Stroke. "Wait."

Methodically, Ms. Jennings ran a rectangular block of depleted uranium along the edge to clean the blade. Ultra-thin strips of the superdense metal curled up from the block and tumbled to the carpeted floor with tiny thumps. The Ginsu people would kill to get hold of that sword. Which is the only way to remove it from the deadly hands of Mindy Jennings.

A minute later, the limo rounded a bend and we saw the exit. Someday, I would have to discover how the hell she did that. Smell the paint on the sign?

On the side of the road was a set of empty wooden stakes, the pale clean wood at the top clearly announcing where a sign had formerly been located. Hmm. Was somebody trying to hide the very existence of the town? Or just sidetrack the idle curious?

Slowing alongside, we were able to see a green and white metallic sign lying partially hidden in the grass. And just beyond was a double line of rubber yellow cones closing off the exit ramp. A brand-new sign said that the road was closed for repairs.

"Isn't this the only route in or out of town?" asked Donaher, tugging on the ends of his long moustache.

Placing an ear against the colored paper, Raul briefly consulted the map. "Yes, it is," he confirmed.

"Oh, Tina!" I called.

A plush recliner swiveled about to display the amazingly buxom Christina Blanco. Wearing only denim shorts, ankle-strap sandals and a skimpy red halter top, the tan actress would have been considered a major traffic hazard in any civilized nation. A recent addition was a tiny tattoo of a butterfly decorating her shoulder. The tattoo used to be on the opposite thigh. I was surprised to learn that butterflies migrate.

Waving her fingers about as if saying goodbye to a friend, the wizard formed trails of sparkling lights in the air.

"*Nyet*, Edwardo," said the statuesque blonde in her heavily accented English. "Bridge intact is."

The lovely Russian mage had only recently joined our covert team and her knowledge of the language was nowhere as good as her command of the occult arts.

With a nod, I loosened both of the .357 Magnums in my double shoulder holster. "Okay, battle stations."

That statement was immediately followed by a series of metallic clacks as a wide variety of weapons was prepped for instant combat. Except, of course, for the two wizards. Gunpowder and magic mix about as well as sex and glue. But each mage held a metallic staff. A master wizard, Raul had a four-foot-long staff made of pure silver. Tina, just a beginner mage, had one of stainless steel. But since she possessed the stolen power of three adult wizards, hers was also four feet in length. Precisely as long as Horta's. Exactly. To the micron. Once in the middle of the night, I had accidentally caught them drunk, in the closet, measuring each like a couple of teenagers.

Mages. They're the main reason antacids were invented.

George awoke.

Wary of a trap, I carefully rotated the steering wheel and maneuvered onto the berm to bypass the safety barrier. Momentarily, a meter on the dashboard flickered, indicating that we were in the process of running over needle-tipped railroad spikes buried in the loose gravel. There was only the faintest burbling noise as our self-repairing tires handled the inconvenience.

As we spent most of our duty time traveling, aside from the standard amenities the massive RV was equipped with: front-launched Amsterdam Mark IV all-purpose missiles, side-mounted .50-caliber machine guns, twin aft 40mm grenade launcher and miniature claymore mines in the door handles. Moreover, the hull could be electrified and the razor-edged door could instantly snap closed under eight thousand pounds of hydraulic pressure. The van could also instantly change color, travel underwater, through fire, and sported a quadriphonic Blough Punk stereo with digital CD player. A true technological marvel, the upholstered fort got terrible gas mileage. Ah well, nothing was perfect.

Maintaining an even speed, the long RV rolled onto the old country bridge, the stout oak beams that constituted the main expanse of the massive trestle rattling and clattering under our twenty-four tons of military armor.

When we reached mid-span, another meter ticked, showing that a device underneath the bridge had just bombarded the van with an EM pulse which should have fried every working circuit in the vehicle.

The wheels started humming again when we reached macadam and I increased the speed, only to hit the brakes. A tree lying across the road blocked any possible advance. It may have only been my imagination, but it was certainly starting to appear as if somebody really didn't want any visitors going to Hadleyville. Maybe tourist season was finished for the spring.

"Brace yourselves," I calmly announced, hitting the buttons for the nitrous-oxide injector and the automatic front jacks at the same time. With a roar, the gigantic van lurched forward and jerked up to bounce over the horizontal oak. We hit the ground with a moderate jar and rolled sedately onward. I tried to hide a smile and failed. God, I love doing that.

Moving at a slow pace, the RV barely crested the next hill

when the road leveled out nicely. A couple of miles later, at the bottom of a low hill, I slammed onto the brakes so hard that Amigo almost went through the windshield. Sprawled in the middle of the road were dozens of dead bodies.

Or rather, what remained of them.

2

Slow and easy, the team exited the van, watching where they stepped so as not to disturb anything of importance on the lonely country road. But with a sick stomach I knew it would be hard to find anything significant in all this blood.

Maybe a dozen corpses dotted the concrete, the limp forms sprawled flat in dry pools of caked brown matter. A buzzing cloud of insects darkened the sky. I had smelled worse, but not in this universe.

There was no sign of their cars.

Jessica started clicking her camera, taking shots of the crime scene. Raul and Tina put their heads together to confer, then majestically waved their wands. Instantly, the cloud of flies went buzzing away and we got a clear view of the bodies.

The corpses had no hands or heads. Yuck.

The last to leave the van, I flipped a switch activating our Dead Man box to record our conversations and armed the self-destruct. If anybody, or thing, tried to enter without our consent—boom.

"Raul, George, do a perimeter sweep," I ordered, Magnum in hand. "Mindy on guard. Jess, photo everything. Tina and Donaher with me."

The team separated to their assigned tasks. George paused only a moment to grab a spare belt of linked .30 ammunition for his banjo.

Pulling a fountain pen from inside his cassock, Donaher removed the cap and telescoped out a long surgical probe. Removing another pen from my own shirt pocket, I twisted the middle twice and gave it to him.

Gazing through my pen, he prodded the ends of an arm and a neck stump. He tried very hard not to step in the blood and almost succeeded. Steeling myself, I went through the pants, shirts and dresses. Every pocket was clean. Not even lint remained. A very professional job.

"Well?" asked Tina after a moment.

"Amateurs," stated the big priest coldly.

Eh? "Explain," I demanded.

"They cut off the hands at the wrist, here, where the joint bones are their thickest," demonstrated Donaher. "A classic beginner's mistake. Plus, while the wrists were done in one shot, the neck took two. I postulate the implement as a wedge of smooth steel, very sharp and thin. A butcher's cleaver would be perfect. Maybe a machete, but it would have to be new."

"How do you know that?" asked Blanco.

"Machetes are manufactured from cheap steel," answered Mindy, stooping over to inspect something on the ground. "They dull fast and resharpening always leaves irregularities in the blade length." Dead bodies didn't bother our martial artist in the least. Lord knows she'd made enough in her time.

Her camera clicking steadily, Jessica gave a shiver. "But why remove the heads and hands? Symbolism? Demonic ceremony?"

"Lunch?" added Horta.

"To hinder identification," said George around the beef stick in his mouth. Hefting his heavy banjo to a more comfortable position, Renault suddenly seemed to realize the food was there, made a face and threw the snack into the weeds.

"Sure be hard as hell to tell who is who, if the fools had also taken the feet along with the wallets and rings," he said, scrubbing his mouth with a handkerchief.

True enough. Footprints were like fingerprints, totally unique, and they never change. We had identified many a weird corpse by processing prints off feet to compare with hospital records taken of babies at birth. It was a long and tedious process, despite the recent augmentation of computers. But it did work. Eventually.

"Besides, they may be . . . wearing the heads as a disguise," I finished. It was a very strange business we were in.

"Appears as if the victims were physically pulled out the windows of their cars," stated Donaher, brushing a tattered coat sleeve. "Note the tiny glass particles on their clothes? And here, and over there, on the road."

Yanked out of the closed window of a moving vehicle? Wow. Our mysterious perps were seriously tough hombres. Even worse than South Philly cops. Curiously, I glanced about for any splotches of green or yellow or black fluids. "Any blood that isn't human?"

"None that I can see."

"Damn."

Standing in the middle of the roadway, I tried to reconstruct the sequence of events in my mind. "Okay. Cars are driving along this road. Something, or things, jump onto the vehicles and pull the drivers out through the windows." I glanced around at the trees and safety barrier. "So how come there are no automobile wrecks? What'd they do? Eat the cars?"

George gave a sharp whistle. "Over here!" he cried, and motioned us closer. "Skid marks!"

Long irregular streaks on the road surface told the story of brakes applied hard. Many of the tracks overlapped each other.

"How many vehicles?" asked Raul as he started pulling off the shoes of a corpse to take toe prints.

"Ten, twelve cars," I estimated.

Tina distorted her face into an expression of disgust. "Which implies many killers."

"Ominous," agreed the other mage, applying a sheet of shiny white paper to the soles of the headless man. The acid in the skin began to form recognizable patterns on the specially treated paper. It wasn't an invention of the Bureau's, just standard FBI-issue field equipment.

With the tip of her sword, Mindy prodded the laurel bushes which edged this section of the road. "They came through here," she announced. "And hid behind this clump of evergreen trees."

"Any details?" growled Donaher, grimly stroking the pump action on his Remington 12-guage shotgun. Father Mike considered killing monsters a holy chore. One he performed with relish.

She squinted at the leaves. "Fifty ... maybe sixty. Humans."

Everybody stopped.

"Humans?" queried George with a frown. "You sure?"

"Dress shoes, high heels, slippers, bare feet, boots and a lot of sneakers," she replied in answer. "This soil is nicely moist and holds the tracks well."

"Sneakers?" queried the big redheaded priest.

Mindy gestured. "Take a look."

Mike and I ambled closer and stared at the dirt. It appeared to be perfectly smooth and unmarred. But what the hey, that's one of the reasons we had Ms. Jennings along. She could follow a drop of rain in a typhoon. I often experienced trouble locating my car keys.

"Hey, Ed," asked Raul, returning from the van. "Do you think it might be some more of the Augmented Men?"

Vehemently, I shook my head. "We killed the last of those schizo mechazoids in Idaho. This is something new and nasty."

"Strange and serious."

"Deadly and dangerous," said George, finishing the slogan.

"And hairy as a hound," added Donaher.

Eh? That wasn't part of the litany.

Using tweezers, the priest lifted a minuscule item from a crimson-splattered shoulder. "Ed, this was done by werewolves!"

The whole team hurried closer, and the long coarse hair was passed around.

"What?"

"Can it ... ?"

"Nyah."

Damnation, this made no sense. Each clue contradicted the others. The marks on the victims appeared to be done by an amateur, yet identification was expertly removed. The tracks were human, tool-using humans, but werewolf hair was on the bodies. Okay, so it was humans, or humanoids, with supernatural strength, speed, agility. But certainly not dumb ol' werewolves. Those idiots driving cars? Using machetes?

"Impossible," snorted Jessica, holding the follicle to the sun. But the stern expression on her face softened into puzzlement. "Ed, werewolves are not sentient. Wolfmen even less so!"

Standing erect, Tina appeared puzzled. "Explain, please. Werewolf, wolfman is not same?"

"Faith, lass, a werewolf is a person who assumes the partial form and abilities of a wolf," explained Donaher lugubriously. "A wolfman is an animal which achieves the partial structure of a human."

"And both are not smart?"

"Never," I stated firmly. "It's only in the movies and bad horror novels that werecreatures chat on the phone or use a fax machine. The best we've ever encountered was a wolfman who figured out how to trigger a rifle. Unfortunately for him, the muzzle was pointing in the wrong direction."

Raul agreed. "Most werewolves are stymied by revolving doors and light switches. It's the lone saving grace in fighting the bastards. Weres are the meanest, toughest, most stubborn, amoral, devious sonsofbitches in this whole dimension."

"Even worse than corporate lawyers?" she asked, amazed.

A nod. "Yep."

Blanco muttered something appropriate in Russian. "So werecreatures stealing wallets is impossible?"

"Ab-so-lutely."

"So how came this to be?"

There she had us stumped.

Lifting my left wrist, I activated my wristwatch, established a relay link with our van and turned on the scrambler circuit.

"Calling Merlin's Tower," I said loud and clear, hoping

the transmission could be heard. The Rocky Mountains were dense enough to foul anybody's communications system.

"This is Merlin's Tower," the Bureau answered. "Identify, please."

"This is Team Tunafish. Report number three for 7/26/91."

"Stardate 4132.96," quipped Raul.

Mindy shushed him.

I shot him a dirty look and continued. "We have a multiple slaying on a country road outside Hadleyville, West Virginia. Indications are that the killing was possibly done by intelligent werewolves and—"

"By *what*?!" crackled my watch.

Bemused expressions came from the team. It was the first time HQ had ever interrupted anybody during a field report.

"Intelligent werewolves," I repeated. "There may be a link between the deaths and the ethereal explosion of yesterday. We will investigate, and report every thirty minutes from this mark." I gave 'em a beep. D-flat, I believe. "If we miss two reports, consider this area a Class Alpha Three hot zone and send in General MacAdams and the Phoenix Squad."

A short whistle of astonishment sounded, but was cut short. Must be a new guy at Communications. "Ah, acknowledged, Tunafish."

"Roger, base. Over and out."

"Over and out," crackled the tiny speaker.

Shaking my watch to terminate the transmission, I grimly reached into a pocket and started screwing a silencer onto the barrel of my Model 42 ultra-lightweight Magnum. The muzzle blast of the heavy-duty Model 66 gave silencers an annoying tendency to explode, which simply ruined my aim. However, I made good-and-goddamn sure both pistols were loaded with blessed silver bullets.

"Okay," I announced, easing the cylinder closed. "The stolen cars will take hours to trace. So let's follow the forest trail. Maybe we can find the transdimensional hole, the flying saucer these things landed in, or whatever caused these freaks."

Steadfast, my team murmured assent.

I clicked back the hammers. "On foot. Standard formation. Single file, one meter spread. Mindy on point. George take the rear."

"Check."

"No problem, Ed."

As we entered the thick array of bushes, I noted a faded sign on the road which boasted: "Welcome to Hadleyville. Population 2,572." Somehow, I doubted the first and wondered about the validity of the second.

The team lost sight of the carnage as we proceeded deeper into the morass of bushes, trees and shrubbery that composed the dense West Virginia forest. In ragged stages, the cool, lush greenery swallowed us whole.

And then it attacked.

3

In a wild explosion of green and brown, the bushes raked at our faces, weeds whipped our legs and trees slammed their limbs towards our heads. Even the very grass under our feet moved trying to trip us. Cursing, my team stumbled into a defensive circle firing every weapon we owned.

"Alex Haley!" I cried, aiming my Magnums for the roots. A thorny vine ripped away the front of my shirt, exposing the molded body armor underneath. As my bullets blasted the vine apart, sticky sap spraying into the air, I made a mental note to get tougher shirts.

"Huey, Dewey and Louie!" shouted George, and we ducked. In a stuttering roar, his banjo began spitting flame. For a single moment, the protective illusion faded to reveal the ungainly M-60 machine rifle in his trained grip. The shiny belt of linked ammunition dangling from the breech mechanism of the huge weapon shrank with alarming speed, but the heavy-duty .30 combat rounds chewed a path of destruction through the attacking foliage.

A prismatic blur, Mindy's sword was out, the long blade flashing with rainbow eagerness. A tree branch thrust close to her and withdrew as kindling. Jessica's camera sprayed pneumatic death at the Spanish moss. Father Donaher's shotgun boomed a hellstorm of hot lead, blowing away bushes, destroying daisies and pulverizing pansies.

". . . !" shouted Raul in the secret language of mages, and a howling blizzard of ice and snow began blasting from the business end of his wizard's staff.

". . . !" added Tina as volcanic flames poured from her

own wand. In deadly harmony, the two mages went back-to-back, and turning round each other, overlapping the zones of their spells. Soon, the nearby greenery was reduced to charred ice statues and dirty snow, with only a muddy band of steaming bare ground encircling us.

As the rest of the forest rustled its leaves in unbridled anger, we caught our breath. Whew. I'd heard about planting a trap, but . . . trapping the plants?

"Thank you, Lawn Doctors Mengele," I said, saluting.

Flushed with excitement, Raul smiled. "No prob, chief-a-roo."

"My pleasure, comrade," added Tina, firing a miniature Lightning Bolt at a suspicious hunk of honeysuckle. It fried.

While reloading my Magnums, I noted that my Bureau-issue sunglasses gave no Kirlian aura reading off these ambulatory plants. There was no white for good, black for evil, green for magic. Nothing! Maybe botanical life was too primitive to register.

"This was a trap," stated Father Donaher, ramming fresh shells into his shotgun. "If the plants had been simply trying to get food, they would have attacked the instant Mindy was among them."

"Instead, they waited for the lot of us." I shivered. Swell.

After cleaning some sap off my sunglasses, I adjusted the focus and gave the combat zone a fast once-over. While the brunt of the dense forest separated us from the van, there was only scattered brush between here and Hadleyville. No details of the place were clearly visible at this range. Just buildings and houses. Interestingly, not a person was running this way to find out what the firefight had been about. Not very surprising, all things considered.

Could the plants have attacked the cars on the highway?

"Should we go back for the RV?" asked Jessica, screwing a telephoto long lens onto her camera.

In scorn, Mindy curled her lip. "Retreat? Never!"

Raul proffered his wristwatch. "I can call Amigo and have him bring the van to us."

"The way that lizard drives?" scoffed George rudely. "No thanks. We're safer with the plants."

"Priority one is getting to Hadleyville," I reminded them, stomping on a dandelion trying to get up my pants leg. "If there are any survivors trapped, they may need immediate evac and medical help."

"Hey, babe, can you conjure some defoliant?" asked George as he removed the tape from the handle of a thermite grenade clipped to his belt. I approved. The time for subtlety was over.

Lovingly, Blanco caressed the short soldier's grim face, making his expression noticeably soften. Ah, young lust. Messy but romantic.

"Da," she purred. "But maybe can do better than that. How far is to town?"

"Hadleyville? About half a mile."

Blanco and Horta started mumbling to themselves in that secret wizard way.

"You've never done it before," warned Raul.

"But you are good teacher."

A cocky smile. "Yep, I am. Okay, go for it."

"Mindy!" called Tina, her staff starting to visibly pulse with power.

Sword in hand, the slim woman turned from slicing apart a particularly determined bit of ragweed. "Yeah?"

"I will be point."

"Be my guest," said Jennings, waving her forward.

After consulting her pocket spell book, Christina started chanting and spinning her staff in the manner of a drum major's baton. Steadily, the speed increased until the wand was only a blur. Then the Russian mage removed her hand and the steel length continued to twirl in place, going faster and faster, until the rod hummed from the sheer raw velocity of its violent rotations.

"Forward," intoned Tina in a Voice of Command, and the staff levitated towards the town.

As the smear advanced, everything in front of us—plants, trees and even rocks—was reduced to flying splinters and dust. Some of the greenery tried to make a run for safety, but each was annihilated. The saps. Single file, we followed the wizard and her wand, staying in the trail of scorched earth behind her. Occasionally, some fanatic bush would try to run close anyway, and we shot it to pieces. Brought a whole new meaning to the word "crabgrass."

As the team progressed, I could only catch an occasional glimpse of the street beyond the row of houses. There did not appear to be any wrecked vehicles or bodies. But I wasn't sure. Definitely a lot of damage to the buildings. Maybe this whole incident was only a horticultural experiment gotten entirely out of control. Or a lunatic killer wearing a bad toupee.

Intelligent werewolves?

Exiting the forest, Tina reclaimed her staff and allowed Mindy to take point again. Only dried mud, gravel and a flimsy wire fence stood between us and Hadleyville. We moved closer. It was a hurricane wire fence, topped with an array of thin wire resting on insulated posts.

"Electrified?" asked Mindy.

"Detection wire," I answered. "Works on proximity. However, with two mages near by—"

Boldly, I touched the wire and nothing happened. The same as with radios, TVs, computers and guns. Mages were just a wet blanket on the fire of technology. Whenever we had to use a commercial airline, getting Raul and Tina past the security scanner was always a royal pain in the butt. We weren't allowed to visit Dulles Airport anymore. And I don't even want to think about the problems we experienced getting cable TV installed!

Set in a sturdy iron-pipe framework, a simple hinged door with a commercially purchased lock barred our use of the fence. A key lock? Trying not to laugh, I reached for a lock-pick in my shirt, but Mindy cut off the restraining bar with a swipe of her sword. The metal pieces tumbled to the ground, the cut ends mirror bright. Raul scanned for magical runes while George checked for booby traps before we swung the gate ajar. It was clean. Beyond the fence was a wide expanse of plush lawn, deep green and smooth as a billiard table. Or was that a pool table? Golf course? Hockey rink? Sports was not my forte.

Sword in hand, Mindy started through the fence.

"Freeze," growled George, his eyes mere slits.

Everybody went motionless.

Silently chewing the inside of his cheek, Renault stared at the manicured lawn. "Ed, got an EMS with you?"

I patted my hip. "Of course."

"Do a full-spectrum scan, will ya?"

What an incredible paranoid the man was. But then, that's how you survive in the Bureau. I once got bit where the sun don't shine because I though a banister was safe to sit on. I had been wrong.

"Natch," I acquiesced.

Reaching into the jacket of my sports coat, I removed a portable electromagnetic scanner and started a general sweep of the lawn. The reading went off the scale.

"Land mines," I cursed, returning the device to my coat.

Assorted noises of displeasure. But we kept it relatively clean, since Donaher was present.

"What kind of mines?" asked Tina Blanco.

Aghast, the big priest stared at her. "Saints above, lass! What kind? The kind that go boom. Are there any others?"

"Who cares?" stated Raul cavalierly, the tiny bells on his yacht moccasins chiming a merry two o'clock. "We're mages. The mines won't go off when we walk on them. So Tina and I will blaze a path for the rest. Okay?"

As the only ex-soldier in the group, George gave me a weary glance that said it all. Civilians!

"Wrong, Mr. Wizard," Renault informed him. "Some mines explode when you step on them. Others when you get near. More detonate when you step on some other mine. Plus, a few wait after being stepped on and then explode later."

"Good gods, why?"

"A delayed blast gets more of the invading group by exploding in the middle of them."

A pause. "Oh."

"And some first ignite a small charge to shoot the huge

secondary charge into the air so it explodes in your face," I added succinctly.

"Or your groin," snarled Renault as a curse. "I know a couple of soprano marines who can testify to that. They're called Bouncin' Bettys."

"The land mines, not the marines," he quickly corrected.

Morally outraged, Father Donaher hawked to spit at the mine field, then paused in reflection and swallowed instead. Wise move.

"So how do we get past them? Circle round to the main road?" asked Jessica, turning along the fence. Suddenly, the bushes and trees in that direction went very still. "No. Never mind. That's probably even better protected than this side exit."

"We could crawl along on our hands and knees probing the soil with a knife like they do in the old war movies," suggested Jennings eagerly, drawing a foot-long butterfly knife from inside her shirt.

"Knifing may work, or it may not," growled George, pulling the big bolt on his M-60. "But this definitely will."

In a thunderous roar, the machine rifle began spraying a stream of armor-piercing rounds into the ground, the big .30 bullets chewing a path through the manicured grass. A few meters out the soil exploded in a geyser of flame. Then again. A bit further out a dark metallic oval boomed into the air and then exploded at chest level. There was another of those, two more geysers, and the bullets began impinging on the wooden fence. In a spray of splinters the clapboard collapsed, offering us a path through to the town.

George released the trigger, and a ringing silence engulfed us. For a moment we all worked our jaws to try and stop the echoes in our ears. Wow. Sensurround, eat your heart out. Even the animated forest seemed temporarily stunned. However, during the bombardment, I had been watching the town. Not a window curtain stirred, nor a light blinked on. Hadleyville appeared totally deserted. Yet, somehow, I had the feeling that we were not alone. Maybe it was only ghosts.

What the hell was this place? Augmented humanoids, animated trees, high-tech proximity sensor wires and a Whitman's Sampler of land mines. What had we stumbled upon here? A lost Bureau 13 base?

In the summer 1977, an unknown foe had decimated the Bureau, killing 90 percent of our operatives in less than four hours. We still had no idea who had done it or why.

Only slightly less important than the identity of the mysterious foe was the fact that a lot of files were lost in the aftermath, including the locations of hundreds of our secret hideouts. Mostly small bolt holes, some only hidden rooms in hotels, the covert locations were used as emergency hideouts or surveillance blinds. Occasionally, a Bureau team relocated a lost base. The sites were usually deserted, sometimes with the bones of the original Bureau agents trapped behind magical doors that would no longer function. But once, we discovered a bolt hole turned into a foul nest for Cherubs of Hate, and another occupied with Tibetan Imperial Bloodslugs, the demonic escargots using Bureau 13 equipment and weapons to seek revenge on the staff of a local French restaurant. I shuddered at the memory of their illustrated menus. It was enough to make a grown man become a vegetarian. Feh.

We reclaimed those bases, but it was never fun.

Pensively, I ran a hand through my hair and scratched the outside of my brain. Could this be one of those scenarios? Was Hadleyville a lost Bureau location? Battling hellspawn armed with our own weapons was every agent's worst nightmare. Every sane agent. However, it was our job.

I eased back the hammers on both Magnums. "Come on, gang, let's go visit beautiful downtown Hadleyville."

In battle formation, we crept across the backyard and angled round the side of the house. That was when we realized why the perspective had been wrong on the building.

There was no front.

Or more correctly, the entire front of the home had been squeezed? . . . smashed? . . . into the rear. The building was only about a foot thick, similar to a Hollywood false front used in a movie. Only the whole structure was there, just compressed.

Before moving past the house, Mindy eased her sword out into the front yard and wiggled it about. When nothing happened, she proceeded onward and one by one the entire team boldly tagged along. In passing, I noticed that the windows weren't even broken. And from somewhere inside, a light was still shining. *Aye caramba.*

Looking uptown and down, we could see that every house on this outer block was mushed the same way. The street was bare of cars, and the homes on the other side seemed okay, just odd somehow. As if it were difficult to focus my vision on them.

"Raul?" asked Tina, just as I was about to.

Thoughtfully, the mage scratched his head with his wand. That made me nervous until I realized that he was only doing it to aid the thinking process. Horta often went into itching fits when in the immediate presence of evil magic. This odd tendency of his had saved our butts more than once.

"Possible," the pale wizard conceded at last. "If Hadleyville is indeed the source of that ethereal explosion, such a reaction as this is, theoretically, possible."

Stepping over a pile of smashed plaster ducks, Donaher held his pocket microscope pen to an accordioned window.

"Could there be survivors?" asked Tina with a spark of hope.

"No way," said the priest flatly. In perfect harmony, the inside light flickered and then faded away.

Bummer.

Ahead of us stretched a flat green lawn and a smooth black driveway made of macadam. Dividing the two was a path of irregularly spaced blue Virginia flagstone. We took the path.

Reaching the sidewalk, I observed that the street was completely empty of cars, and incredibly clean. The black asphalt seemed brand-new, just like the driveway, without a Popsicle stick, leaf or newspaper in evidence. Nor any potholes. That was suspicious. Potholes were the official state animal of West Virginia.

With George and Tina flanking her, Mindy stepped off the curb and onto the street, her eyes constantly moving in search of danger. But as her sneaker touched the hard macadam, the material parted in a watery manner, and with a blub, she sank out of sight.

4

Dropping my guns on the crumpled lawn, I insanely reached out, grabbed hold of the lowering blade of Mindy's sword and, bracing myself with both legs, yanked backwards with every ounce of strength I possessed.

Pain!

Trembling and sweaty, I came awake sitting on the grass with an oily black form lying nearby. It was roughly human-shaped, with the bloody end of a sword sticking out of one end. Chanting wildly, Raul lowered the end of his staff and a steamy discharge bathed the deadly quiet form of our friend. For a moment, the body was completely masked, then as the billowing fumes dispersed, Mindy groaned and struggled to sit upright.

"Blah," she said, and spat black onto the sidewalk.

Like a living snake, the ebony fluid undulated along the concrete and into River Street.

As the team gathered close, I glanced at my hands. There was a pink line across each palm and on every finger in a staggered pattern. When I closed my hands, the pattern joined to form a straight line. Warily, I flexed my hands expecting agony. But everything felt fine.

"You have the good father to thank," said Jess, offering me a hip flask.

Unscrewing the cap, I took a healthy swallow. Ah, ten-year-old blended Kentucky whiskey. Now, that was a Healing spell.

"Thank Donaher for what?" I asked, returning the flask.

She stuffed the container into her camera bag. "Tina magically healed your wounds, but when one of your

49

thumbs was rolling away, Mike made a catch just before it reached the street."

Wow. Talk about giving a fellow a hand.

As I struggled to my feet, an amazingly clean Mindy came over and grabbing my coat lapels, proceeded to administer a kiss that could only be measured in amperes of high voltage. Something around the gigawatt range.

"Thank you," she said afterwards.

Embarrassed, I retrieved my Magnums lying on the ground and wiped some blood spots off the handles.

"So how do we get across the street of death?" asked Father Donaher, brushing out his moustache. "Build a raft?"

Jessica chuckled. "Thank you, Huck Finn."

"We can fly," offered Raul, raising his staff.

Mages! They would use magic to open soda cans and then be actually surprised when they ran out of power in the middle of a battle. Sheesh!

"No, we need a bridge," I told him, scanning the horizon.

Donaher tapped the barrel of his shotgun against a nearby telephone pole. "How 'bout this?"

"Perfect," I acknowledged, drawing my ultra-lightweight Magnum. Removing the silencer, I assumed a regulation firing stance and snapped off six shots, neatly cutting the wires free from the crossbars of the pole. We Wyoming boys were born with a pistol in one hand and a beer in the other. Which explained why my penmanship was so bad.

Most of the wires slumped to the ground, but one line fell to dangle into the street. There ensued a brutal tug-o'-war which ended with the cable snapping off from the pole and whipping into the macadam like a strand of spaghetti.

Having seen worse, we were unimpressed. Once my team spent an entire summer stationed in Detroit.

"Ms. Jennings?" I requested, stepping aside.

Shifting her hips, Mindy's sword went through the telephone pole to no apparent result. Then the thick pole slid apart on a sharp angle and toppled over to loudly crash onto the far sidewalk with pinpoint precision.

The street bubbled with anger. Hmm.

"Raul, Tina, maybe you'd better fly over as escort," I instructed the mages. "Just in case."

Gripping her staff, Blanco gave a nod and levitated into the air, while Horta started running towards the sky as if ascending an invisible staircase. The big show-off.

One at a time, we crossed over. Mindy skipped across as if she were on the balancing beam in the gym. Father Donaher slowly shuffled along, refusing to lift a foot from the surface of the pole. Holding his big M-60 machine rifle in both arms to aid his balance, George reached the far side with no problem. Jessica simply strolled along, while I scooted on hands and knees. It was undignified but efficient. Especially since I can't swim.

Halfway across, I noted the pair of fins moving along the macadam surface. Snorting my contempt, I continued on to join the group. Piffle. It was only a transdimensional shark. You could kill 'em with a standard bazooka. Big deal.

Skirting the houses, we scrambled over a backyard fence and found ourselves on the outer rim of a blast crater. Or at least, I couldn't think of anything else to call the pit. The obvious question was, Had the center of town magically exploded outward, or had the whole place gone boom and only the center of town been shielded from the blast?

Hadleyville spread out before us, reduced to layers of concentric bands. At our feet was a ring of jumbled wilderness: machines and plants haphazardly piled together in pure chaos. Next was a circle of bubbling glass. But inside that was an island of normalcy: orderly streets, undamaged homes and in the far distance a shopping mall with a mirrored building. However, I was starting to believe that in this goofy place the more normal something appeared, the greater the danger was. The first fluffy teddy bear I encountered was getting a grenade in the kisser.

Checking my sports coat, I found my long-range folding binoculars and trained them on the Hadleyville Hotel, a modest ten-story building with a nice neon sign announcing a heated swimming pool, color TV in every room and happy hour at the Kon Tiki Lounge every Friday at six. Pou-Pou platter was extra.

But to my sunglasses there was a steady ethereal wind whirling round the upper structure of the building. Purple lightning crackled against the bloated crimson clouds that moved under their own volition. A thick coat of primordial ooze dripped down the sides of the eerily twisting building, while dark muted shapes moved with inhuman purpose behind warped windows misty with cold yet moist with glowing slime.

The parking lot was a smooth expanse of empty black macadam. I could guess what happened to the cars. I'm surprised the lot wasn't burping with a giant toothpick sticking out of its entrace ramp.

"Hey, there's an electronic crawl sign over by the Kon Tiki Lounge," announced Jessica, fine-focusing her pocket binoculars. "Welcome . . . to the . . ." She dropped the binoculars. "Oh no."

"What?" I demanded, trying to find what she had.

"Welcome to the First International Occult Convention of Hadleyville," she read in a tiny voice.

Hoo boy.

"What now, comrade?" asked Tina, concerned. "Should we attack? Call for assistance? Run away?"

I seriously debated that. "Not yet. We haven't encountered anything really dangerous. Let's go further. Our answers should be in that hotel."

"Agreed," said Donaher. His oversize gold crucifix was held in both hands before him in a defensive position. "I sense great evil there. Yet everything inside is not evil."

"Fabulous," moaned Jennings. "Some innocent bystander hiding in a closet, I suppose."

Jessica frowned. "Is it a trapped desk clerk?"

George snapped the bolt on his M-60. "A hostage? Sacrifice?"

"I cannot say for certain," murmured the priest. "But I strongly suggest we proceed with extreme caution."

"All is not as it seems," he added softly.

George tilted his head to gaze upward at the moaning structure. "Anybody got a clever idea how we can find out what happened inside the hotel?" he asked.

Ghostly figures moved in and out of the pulsating walls, while blood started to run out of one window to be licked up by another. The front door was full of sharp teeth, and a fleshy tongue-like carpet lay panting on the concrete side-walk.

Drawing the Model 66, I checked the scenario load: armor-piercing shell, silver bullet, blessed wooden bullet, mercury-tip explosive round, phosphorus incendiary slug and a hollow-point dumdum. Good enough. I was loaded for were. "Sure," I said, easing back the hammers until they clicked into firing position. "We go inside."

"I was afraid you'd say that," mumbled Renault. "Want me to stay here and guard our escape route?"

"Nope."

"I'll help," offered Tina kindly.

"Sorry. Need you both to administer smelling salts in case I faint."

Smiling, Mindy playfully punched the plump gunner on the arm. "Come on, guys. How often do we get to march into the jaws of death incarnate?"

"Total so far, or this year alone?" queried Raul.

"Sissy," she sneered in contempt.

He stood erect. "And proud of it."

Without warning, Raul jerked backwards and fell sprawl-ing to the ground. A heartbeat later an echoing *cra-ack!* of a large-caliber rifle rolled over us.

"Jules Verne!" I bellowed as the rest of my team headed for the center of the earth.

"Pink Floyd!" added Father Donaher, ramming shells into his shotgun.

Only Blanco was still standing.

"Pink Floyd?" she repeated, puzzled, as hot bullets zinged by. "Dark Side of the Moon? Wish you were here?"

"The Wall!" croaked Horta, and gesturing from his prone position, a chest-high barrier of shimmering ethereal energy formed. Four more rifle rounds noisily richocheted off the magical shield.

"Are you okay?" asked Jessica in concern. Edging closer, she yanked apart the top of her camera bag and pulled out a medical kit and plastic bottle of Healing potion #4. It was the good stuff, strictly reserved for emergencies only.

Tugging at the ragged hole in his starry black T-shirt, Horta frowned as the molded body armor underneath came into view. There was a gray metallic smear directly above his heart. "Hey, they completely obliterated the Orion nebula!"

"He's fine," announced Jess, closing the bag.

"Okay, then, on my mark!" I growled, rising to a crouching position. "One . . . two . . . three . . . go!"

In unison, the team stood and emptied our weapons at the distant foes. Since we were armed with pistols and such, they were eminently safe from our retaliation. It was mostly for morale, but what the hey.

Only Father Donaher didn't join the volley discharge. As a Catholic priest he was forbidden, under any circumstance, to take a human life. Technicalities. Technicalities.

"Are you people nuts!" admonished Mindy. "Using short-barreled pistols at an unseen target over two hundred meters away?"

In a shatter of glass, a screaming figure crashed out of the upper windows of the hotel and tumbled to the hard pavement ten stories below. From the reaction, it appeared that the concrete was very hard and most unfriendly at this time of year.

"Of course, there's always blind luck," she relented.

"Divine providence," corrected Donaher.

George grunted. "Thought that was in Rhode Island."

"Heathen."

"Democrat," corrected Renault.

"Same thing."

Just then a thin finger of flame stretched out from the hotel and impacted on the barrier with pyrotechnic results.

"What in the . . . that was a LAW rocket!" stormed George, untangling the feed of the ammo belt to his M-60. "Who are these guys?"

I retrieved my sunglasses from the dirt. "Let's find out."

Adjusting the focus with my Donaher thumb, I found the hotel and trailed upward until I located our attackers on the top floor. Long rifle barrels protruded from open windows and I got a fine clear view of them: two men and a woman.

Then the world went very still. Because through the Kirlian-sensitive lenses, I could also see the aura of the normally invisible tattoo on their foreheads. A very famous tattoo. The design of a dagger through the moon.

"It's the Scion," I announced as calmly as possible.

At the base of the hotel, the smashed body stood as a large hairy form and dashed inside the hotel.

"And they're the werewolves."

More bullets came our way.

"The Scion?" asked Tina.

And I explained. The Scion of the Silver Dagger was a lunatic organization dedicated to destroying the world for no particular reason that we have ever been able to discover. Sort of a dark version of the Bureau, they practiced voodoo, witchcraft, black magic, ate human flesh and were generally considered on the level of something to scrape off your shoe before entering a house.

"Saints preserve us!" cried Father Donaher, smacking his forehead. "Ed, this isn't a lost Bureau base, it's one of theirs!"

Yeow! What a notion.

"It certainly would explain the weird offensive devices we encountered," commented Renault dryly as he fingered the Colt .45 at his belt. "Who else but the Scion would have killer crabgrass and military weapons?"

"Who indeed?" quipped Mindy, her hands twisting on the pommel of her sword.

"But what is the Scion of the Silver Dagger doing with an occult convention?" asked Jessica petulantly, her camera clicking steadily. "Holding a recruiting drive?"

On command, we stood, fired and crouched again.

"A possibility," I acknowledged while reloading. "They certainly have suffered a lot of personnel losses recently. Especially after their massive failure with the Forever Castle."

"True enough."

Another LAW hit the shimmering barrier.

I yawned to pop my ears back into working order.

"An occult convention where something went horribly wrong. Or, worse, something went horribly right."

Mindy blinked, and shook her head. "Causing Hadleyville to be destroyed, and every surviving member of the Scion transformed into a werewolf."

"A sentient werewolf."

"Feh."

I agreed. Feh on toast. With ketchup.

"Raul, how long can you hold this barrier?" asked George, laying an assortment of grenades on the ground. Father Donaher was doing the same, and Mindy was hastily assembling a compound bow from her pocket arsenal of secret ninja deathdealers. Patent pending.

Spreading powders on the dirt in a rune pattern, the mage loftily sniffed his disdain. "Against purely physical weapons? No problem. Domes take a lot of power. Globes even more so. But this? Piffle."

Father Donaher blinked, and shook his head. "Piffle? Now, where did he learn language like that?"

A thumb jerk. "From Ed, of course."

I was shocked. "Now, just a doggone minute there, buckaroo—"

Shouting something incomprehensible, Tina stood, and from her cupped hands there lanced a swirling cone of lightning and boiling flame. But the lambent outpouring of concentrated Death spells thinned into nothingness before it reached the hotel. The distance was just too great. And neither wizard could stand long enough to draw the size pentagram necessary to cast a long-distance conjure.

Cra-ack! Zing!

George blinked, and shook his head. "Up yours," he growled.

Jessica stared at him intently.

Activating my wristwatch, I got only a carrier-wave buzz. Interference from the hotel must be blocking the radio signals. And every telepath was off-line. Damn. So much for summoning air support. A renovation via saturation bombing was just what this place needed.

Mindy blinked, and shook her head.

Cra-rack! Zing! Whoosh . . . Boom!

Wisely, I decided it was time to get tough. "Tina, take Donaher and Jessica and teleport back to the limo for our combat armor and heavy-weapons trunk."

Tina blinked, and shook her head. "*Da*, Edwardo."

I blinked, and shook my head. What had I been about to say? Oh yes. "Donaher, assist her with the big—"

Diving forward, Jessica grabbed at Renault and jerked backwards. As she came clear, I could see that my darling wife was holding the pull rings from a brace of grenades.

Frantically, George clawed at his chest. There was an explosion and everything went black.

5

I came awake with both of my .357 Magnums out and searching for danger. Who? What? Where? Ah.

"Hello, dear," said Jess from behind the wheel of the van. We were speeding along a highway somewhere. Sprawled on the rear couches was the rest of the team. Nobody seemed hurt and our weapons were readily evident.

"Hi, hon," I mouthed around a flannel tongue. Then as my head cleared, memories flooded in, and I coldly aimed the Smith & Wessons at the love of my life. If the human sitting near me was Jessica. Her aura read human norm. But that wasn't good enough.

"Holmes," I demanded. If she gave the wrong answer, I would have to move fast after blowing her head off to grab the wheel and keep us from crashing. Luckily, the road was fairly even and straight. I didn't think we were in West Virginia anymore. Ohio?

A rueful smile. "Watson. My, my, aren't you a Mr. Paranoid."

Ain't that the truth? But that was only because I had so many enemies. And they were everywhere. "Mother's maiden name?"

She sighed. "Yang-wu. And I was born in Camden."

"What happened in Honolulu?"

"We ran out of massage oil." Jess cocked an eyebrow. "Satisfied?"

"Yeah, sorry," I said, reholstering my weapons and feeling slightly foolish.

A shrug. "That's okay, Ed. Business is business."

True enough. While it was not an everyday occurrence for my wife to kidnap the team, clones and doppelgangers were a common danger in our line of work. And someday, it wouldn't be my wife I would wake up to. Which would put me in big trouble on two counts.

Just then a sign flashed by my window stating the mileage to the Indiana border. Wow. How long had we been asleep?

"So, what happened?" I asked, reclining in the front seat.

"Gas grenades," she explained.

"That explains the lovely cat litter flavor in my mouth."

"Hey, I don't make 'em. I just use 'em."

Abruptly, Mindy sat up.

"Oh, it was a gas grenade," said Jennings. She chewed her tongue. "Ick. What a taste. I'll start some tea." And she moved off towards the tiny kitchenette.

Sounding like a foghorn on steroids, Father Donaher gave a yawn that threatened to implode the windows. "What the . . . ah, of course. Anesthesia gas."

"Tea?" asked Jennings.

"Please. Thank you."

Stretching his arms to the ceiling, George really put the stress test on his army shirt, and for a moment you could see the hard muscle underneath his fat. His jacket was lying on the floor, and Amigo was half inside one of the pockets munching loudly on what sounded like cookies or bones.

"Geez, Jess," yawned Renault. "You could have asked me for the K47L cans."

"Sorry," sang out my wife. "There was no time."

Damnation! Had everybody figured this out but me?

Tina wobbled erect and ran fingers through her long hair in a crude ablution. "Sleep gas," she rumbled. "Bleh."

On cue, Raul groaned into life. "Oh God, I hate knockout gas," he moaned. "What's the chance of getting a beer?"

"Ed?" asked Mindy, glancing my way.

I nodded yes. Mages had a tendency to drink heavily, and we had to monitor them. On the other hand, absolutely nothing cleared the biochemical crud from your mouth like a frothy cold brew. Except, perhaps, another cold frothy brew.

The door to the small refrigerator opened and a six-pack started to float out.

"One each," I clarified.

Two beers broke free from the levitating pack and wafted

over to Raul and Tina. Now, that's what I call a light beer. The wizards formally clinked containers and drank from the closed cans. I was unimpressed, having seen the Invisible Straw trick before.

After serving George and Donaher, Mindy passed a couple of steaming ceramic mugs to us, and I held the wheel for a moment while Jess added mint and lemon. I took mine straight.

"Okay," I said after a preliminary sip. "Report. How did we get into the limo?"

Jessica lifted a plain copper bracelet into view. "I used this magic bracelet taken from Raul to teleport us to the van."

Wiping the moisture off his hand, Horta accepted the bracelet and slid it back on his wrist. The copper band was drained at present, but the Recharge spell was a minor matter. Raul could do such things in his sleep, and often did. Which explained why nobody ever bothered the wizard during naptime.

"Why the improvisational retreat?" asked Donaher, placing aside his empty mug.

Neatly, my wife maneuvered around an eighteen-wheeler full of livestock. Thank God for air-conditioning.

"Had to," she explained as we accelerated past the portable barn. "We were being systematically mind-probed. And by an expert. Somebody so good that you guys weren't aware that it was happening."

"Then, how did you?" asked Mindy bluntly.

Here Jessica faltered. "I . . . used to do it often enough that I can recognize the signs."

There was a respectful moment of silence from the team.

Until only a few months ago, my lovely bride had been the top telepath in the Bureau—i.e., the world. But after battling a fledgling god, she had been blasted into a normal human. She still possessed an endemic memory, but her vaunted telepathic powers were gone forever. And nothing in Heaven or Hell could make them return. This I knew for a fact, as I had asked the management of both places. Personally.

Would it be the same as one of us going blind or deaf? I didn't know. Nobody but another telepath could know. And I could only ponder on the fact that all of her fellow mentalists were now dead, and it was only her debilitating handicap that allowed her to survive. What was my lady feeling deep down inside. Remorse? Shame?

Envy?

Impulsively, I reached out to touch her, and Jess shied away, her features an iron mask of neutrality. It was at that precise instant that I finally realized exactly how much my wife missed her telepathic abilities.

"Well, if the situation ever occurs again, let's code-name your tactic quote, Friendly Fire, end quote," I suggested, returning my hand to my own lap. "That way, if you're a bit slower, and one of us is a bit faster, we can avoid those nasty laundry bills."

"Agreed."

George turned his head from looking out the window. "Jessica, exactly where are we going?"

"Nowhere," she replied.

"Faith, lass, and why are we going nowhere?" asked Donaher, puzzled.

My wife jerked a thumb backwards. "Them," she said.

Reaching down, I jerked the lever underneath my seat and swiveled about. Amid the rest of the meager traffic, there was a couple of perfectly normal eighteen-wheel Mack trucks behind us.

In a standard #2 surveillance formation.

Oh fudge.

Father Donaher started reciting a prayer of protection.

Tina splayed a golden light from her wand about the van, checking our defensive seals, and George activated the Hummer unit, a nifty little techno-device we got from the CIA. It made our car windows vibrate in an irregular ultrasonic pattern so that anybody using a maser beam couldn't hear our voices through the glass. Also did a damn fine personal massage.

"They've been following us since we departed West Virginia," announced Jess, confirming the suspicion. "I decided not to tell you about them until everybody got a chance to recover from the sleep gas. Let you acclimatize."

I growled annoyance, even though it was good sense. I had almost shot my wife upon awakening. If she had been frantically yelling that we were being trailed by enemy forces . . .

"Any hostile moves?" asked Mindy, her sword out and ready.

"Nope. But where I go, they go."

Sliding back a panel in the ceiling, Mindy liberated a pair of binoculars from the overhead weapons rack.

"The trucks appear to be perfectly ordinary tractor-trailer assemblies," she announced, staring out the window. "A high-riding six-wheel cab, with twelve-wheel trailers being pulled along behind. Different colors and different ages. Sides made of unpainted corrugated steel. No perceptible openings, presumably a double door in the back. One has a compressed gas cylinder on the bottom. Must be refrigerated. There's a variety of company names on the trucks, and ICC numbers. Looks like a simple buddy convoy. Possibly a couple of independent truckers out on a TSD or piecemeal run."

"Faith, lass, I agree," said Father Donaher. "Now, could you try that again in English?"

"They look clean," the former resident of New Jersey explained for everyone's benefit. "No obvious armaments."

"Doesn't mean a damn thing," I noted, clicking the safeties off both my handguns.

"Any CB activity?" asked Raul, polishing his wand with a vengeance. Sparks flew from the tip and arced down into the bottom as the staff charged itself for action.

"Go ahead and try," offered Jess.

Rising from the middle couch, Renault stepped past the wizards and took the swivel chair at the communications panel. He flipped some switches, and a strident howl whined from the floorboard speakers. Scrunching his face in concentration, Renault twisted the dial to different positions and pressed some preset buttons to the same result.

"Full-spectrum jamming," he cursed, savagely twisting the Off dial. "That's the Scion. Subtle as a brick through a window."

"And just as smart," Raul added.

"Did not know our radios could be jammed," puzzled Blanco.

I answered her. "Anybody's radio can be jammed with enough raw power."

"And if they're knocking us off the air, there must not be a working TV or radio station in this whole section of the state!"

"Which means help is on its way," said Tina optimistically. "Bureau will detect and send recon unit." Then her face clouded. "*Nyet.* We are recon unit."

Rotating around, George held out a hand and Donaher tossed him the banjo-from-Hell. Catching the thirty pounds in one hand, our plump soldier worked the bolt on his huge M-60, starting a new belt of ammunition.

"Gas situation?" he asked, already starting to talk in short battlefield sentences.

Jess pointed at the dashboard. "Already on emergency tanks."

Oh swell. Damn this Detroit monster and its low mileage! Didn't Toyota make any armored recreational vehicles?

Crouched over the weapons locker, Father Donaher wiggled his black cloth bottom as he rummaged in an ammunition drawer. "Hey, George! Aren't there any deer slugs for my shotgun?"

"Sure. Over by the Armburst."

"Ah, there they are. Thanks."

Double-ought buckshot cartridges from the good father's Remington could cut most monsters in half. However, the effectiveness of a shotgun is decreased geometrically with distance. That was why he wanted the deer slugs. Simply put, they were bullets for a shotgun. Only the mighty Donaher could handle the mind-numbing recoil of the projectiles, but they changed his shotgun from a short range to a long-range weapon and increased its destructive power astronomically.

As this was plainly no time for trick cameras, I loaded Jess an Uzi machine pistol from the small arsenal in the glove compartment. Maintaining speed, she accepted the weapon, along with four additional clips of mixed ammo. The open carton of grenades I put on the couch for easy access to both of us.

"Mindy, what does radar say?" asked Blanco, the big blonde sliding tiers of copper bracelets from her wizard's kit onto her slim tan arms.

Glancing over my shoulder at the dashboard, the short woman consulted the beeping screen.

"That there are two of them," Jennings announced.

Ah, modern technology. Ain't it grand?

That was when I noticed that both mages were now dressed for warfare in combat sneakers, denim pants, T-shirts and short vest with a zillion tiny pockets bulging with magical items. Of course, Raul's T-shirt was adorned with a giant bull's-eye target surrounded by the international "No" symbol, and on Tina's was a picture of her wearing a T-shirt with a picture of her wearing a T-shirt with a picture of her wearing a T-shirt, ad infinitum, but that was only to be expected.

In grim satisfaction, Father Donaher stroked his Remington shotgun into readiness. "And what's the magical report?" asked the big priest.

"Magical probes show clear," reported the mage as he fondled the empty air before him. "No cargo, one driver per truck."

That caught everybody's attention. The Scion sent two guys riding empty trucks after us when we escaped from their secret headquarters? Bullshit.

With renewed interest, Mindy located her binoculars on the wheels. "Riding too damn low for empties," she observed. "Could be bad suspension on one, but both?"

Adjusting my sunglasses, I dialed for computer enhancement. The view fragmented, the middle section magnifying the lead white cab. Everything seemed normal. They ap-

peared to be just a bunch of tired-looking asphalt jockeys.
Typical long-distance truckers. Following Bureau procedure, I switched to ultraviolet on my sunglasses. Nothing of
interest showed. However, on infrared there were strong indications of heat sources in both trucks. Both of the empty
trucks. Including the refrigeration rig.

"They're phonies," I calmly announced, and that was
when the trucks behind us exploded.

6

The tiny metal squares that had formed the truck walls fluttered in a cloud to the ground, exposing an inner framework of metal struts. Fluted ramps extended from the sides of flatbeds, hovering inches above the rushing concrete, and giants on motorcycles poured onto the turnpike, skillfully scattering to give their brethren room to descend.

The hairy riders had leather bandoliers of ammunition crisscrossing their herculean chests, full-body military flak jackets and oversize crash helmets. Each monster biker was armed with a MAC-10 spray-and-pray and a LAW rocket launcher. Those were big trouble. Enough of those antitank weapons just might prove effective against the armor of the RV. And what was worse, the lunatics weren't riding standard motorcycles, but ultra-fast racing bikes with V-nosed prows, stabilizer fins and studded tires. On or off the road they could easily outrun the heavy van. But what really caught our attention was the innocent-appearing saddlebags draped over the rear fender of every bike. Saddlebags protected by a defensive rune that visibly glowed with power. Made my eyes water just to stare at the things. And my Kirlian sunglasses gave a reading so black with evil it was as if the riders were in a coal-dust cloud.

On my request, Raul and Tina concentrated their magical probes on those lumpy leather pouches. Each was jammed full of C3, the unstable and temperamental grandfather of modern-day C4, high-explosive military plastique. Uh-oh. Fast, I hit the controls for external microphones and video cameras. The back window frosted over to a magnified view of our surprise guests.

· · ·

"Yee-haw!" screamed a grinning slab of muscles, his long body hair flying in the wind. "About time we attacked!"

A heavily scarred werewolf brushed his whiskers with a clawed paw. "Our sorcerer had to finish these bikes first, fool."

Magical motorcycles? I didn't like the sound of that.

"Freaking, deacon," laughed a crewcut werewolf, revving her supercharged 40cc engine to near overload. "On these those Bureau bastards will never escape us again!"

"What if they teleport?"

"Deudonic shields are up to stop them," laughed another.

I glanced at Raul and he nodded glumly. Damn!

"SOBs deserve to die!" shouted a man-monster, an ear dripping with feathers. "Everybody deserves to die!"

"Yowsa!" howled the muscleboy, flipping back and balancing the motorcycle onto its rear wheel. "I'm gonna eat me some Pentagon porkchops! Washington white meat! Federal—"

"Nothing fancy," ordered a big werewolf, his fur having a slight touch of mange. "Let's hit 'n' git!"

The slab wildly shook his head, lashing himself with his own mane. "No! I wanna eat some of them first!"

"Alive?"

"Of course!"

Another laughed. "You wanna eat everything!"

"Not if it looks like you, fuzzball!"

"Enough!" ordered the front werewolf, extending the launch tube of his LAW as a prelude to firing. "Time to get nasty!"

The trucks dropped back, and the motorcycle pack grouped into an attack formation. A shiny metal tidal wave, they surged forward.

"Trouble. We are in trouble," cursed Jessica, holding the Uzi firm between her thighs and yanking on the spring bolt to chamber the first automatic round.

"Battle stations," I shouted, and the Armorlite glass of the rear window became illuminated in a vector graphic of holographic squares as an aid to targeting.

As Jessica urged the van on to even greater speeds, Father Donaher passed out flak jackets, George began activating the scientific defensives of the RV and Mindy laid out medical supplies and started sharpening her sword. Meanwhile, Raul and Tina were throwing colored powders about the RV and chanting as if our very lives depended on their spells.

Finished loading and priming my own personal weapons, I worked the radar trying to get a more detailed reading of our unusual adversaries. They were proof to magic. Had the Scion considered shielding themselves against technology? Nope!

"We have eighty-five bogeys confirmed," I announced in a crisp voice. "Range: three quarters of a klick and closing fast."

Shocked murmurs rose from the team. That many?

"Jess, any chance of outrunning those bikes off the highway?" asked Raul, mixing vials of bubbling chemicals.

"Zero," answered my wife brusquely, concentrating on her driving.

"What about on the highway?"

"Almost zero."

"So, stay on the highway."

"Thank you, Albert Einstein," she said between clenched teeth as we zigzagged through traffic.

The digital speedometer blinked 145-146-147 mph. Cars flashed past us at an increasing pace. Only then did it occur to me that we were butt-deep in civilians. Crap!

"We need combat room," said Father Donaher, obviously thinking along the same lines. "Ed, should I release the oil slick, or the nail-clusters?"

I vetoed both. "Too great a chance of the cars going out of control and crashing into each other. Where's the EMP pistol?"

"We left it in the station wagon," Mindy reminded me.

"Damn!"

Leveling her wand in a grip similar to playing billiards, Tina pointed the steel staff out the window and jerked it forward a nudge. Instantly, the car alongside us faltered and began to slow as its engine conked out. Then the vehicle behind it began to swing around and Blanco got that one also.

"Good shooting, Tex," complimented Horta, picking off a Subaru, Volvo and Pinto in a neat three-banked shot.

Closing an eye in concentration, she only grunted in acknowledgment. Another nudge, and a station wagon full of nuns stalled. Father Donaher doffed an imaginary hat as the puzzled sisters rolled backwards past us.

Together, the mages neutralized engines until there was a solid line of dead cars, vans, and such coasting to a stop behind our van, and getting further behind with every second. Some smart-ass tried to get by on the berm, another on the grassy median, and they also got the Big Stall. Sputter . . . shudder . . . wheeze . . . cough . . . *clunk!*

Then the barrier of cars shook, windshields cracking, as a wave of motorcycles bounded over them in tight formation. The bikes hit the pavement hard but stayed upright, revving their massive engines to full throttle.

The distance between us began to shorten with alarming speed.

Tina and Raul tried the same trick with these guys, but nothing happened. I would have been very surprised to learn that the Scion hadn't magically protected their bikes from such an obvious ploy. The members of the Scion of the Silver Dagger were insane but not stupid. Unfortunately. Sure would have made our job easier if they were.

Barely perceptible, the sixteen-cylinder motor under our hood lowered its screaming output.

"Jess, why the hell are you slowing?" I demanded.

Both hands tight on the wheel, she pointed with her chin. "The cars ahead of us are too damn close! We have got to get more room!"

Great. Swell. Wonderful. "George!"

His chair turned around. "Yeah, Ed?"

"Buy us some time."

A shrug. "Okay." Swiveling to the fire control board, he

threw a few switches and shoved a gangbar to its furthest
setting.

"On my mark, Jess," he said, face tight against a hooded
viewer. "Ready . . . set . . . go!"

Tortured tires squealing and smoking, Jess swerved the
van to a strategic position midway on the road and enticingly
slowed, bringing the oncoming motorcycle pack within opti-
mum range of its weapons. Then the heavy RV began fish-
tailing and the aft .50 machine guns hidden in our tail fins
cut loose, the big copper-jacketed bullets sweeping through
the motorcycle pack. On and on, Renault poured hundreds,
thousands, of rounds at our hairy enemies in a seemingly
endless fusillade. Windshields shattered, and several riders
doubled over, clutching their stomachs. But as we had no silver bullets in the hopper, not a werewolf fell, not a bike
slowed.

Finally, our reserves of ammo became exhausted and the
guns fell silent. Although seriously rattled, the Scion bikers
maintained formation and kept coming. But now both the
cars in front and behind us had enough of a lead to be relatively safe.

"It's showtime," announced Mindy at a control board,
and, flipping the top of a joystick, she pressed the red button
inside.

The phony pile of luggage atop the van dropped its rear
flap and out whooshed a pair of Amsterdam heat-seeking
missiles. Caught by surprise, the werewolves were too
stunned to react. Zeroing in on the red-hot engines, the Am-
sterdams dipped and leveled smooth. Seconds later, a series
of resounding explosions annihilated a goodly portion of the
dogs of war. Pieces of hairy corpses flew everywhere. Our
aft machine guns may not have had silver bullets in their
load, but our missiles sure did!

Struggling to regroup, the remaining bikers retaliated with
their machine pistols clumsily hosing the rear of the RV.

Mindy sent three more rustling firebirds from the nest to
add to the flaming ruin on the road.

A score of badly aimed LAW rockets streaked past us to

violently impact on the highway, geysering flame and throwing tons of concrete skyward.

Far ahead, the disappearing traffic was apparently trying to perform a mass audition for the Indy 500. Good for them.

A few more shots were exchanged with little additional damage done when a lucky shot from the Scion landed inside the missile pod on our roof. Instantly, the volatile cargo of spare missiles detonated in a blinding thunderclap. The baggage rack blew into a million pieces, and the flames spread downward from tiny cracks in the ceiling armor to fill the inside of the limo car. Automatic extinguishers in the walls and seat backs spewed fire-retardant foam everywhere and the blazing carpet was quickly smothered. Coughing from the acrid fumes, I somehow managed to eject the missile launcher. It hit the road in a crash. With hot shrapnel zinging everywhere, the bikers still expertly wheeled around the raging inferno on the highway.

Accepting something from George, Father Donaher tossed it out the window.

"Sick 'em, me boyo!" he cried.

Amigo?

Tumbling through the air, the tiny lizard hit the pavement and bounced directly into the exploding missile pod. Half of the Scion had passed when from out of the roaring flames there appeared a huge reptilian figure. Metamorphosed into his true form, the baby dragon spread his iridescent wings, shrugging off the mass of burning metal. Cawing a war cry, the *enfant terrible* lumbered straight into the motorcycle pack and extended his splayed claws. Moving fast, Amigo managed to snatch six of the werewolves off their bikes and stuff them into his gaping maw.

Horrified, the rest of the Scion veered well past the dragonette, careful to stay far outside his deadly reach, and continued on, leaving the frustrated juggernaut behind at 150 miles per hour. Filling his lungs, Amigo blasted them with a lance of brimstone flame, then started after us in his infant's waddle. It had been a good try.

As the vents heroically struggled to cleanse the air, the Scion regrouped and fired a volley of rockets past us. The rockets exploded in front of the RV, issuing countless volumes of brackish smoke that clung to the hull of the car as we sailed through.

"Nerve gas!" cursed George, watching a meter on the environmental board hit the red line.

I glanced at the cracked ceiling. Only our velocity was keeping the deadly gas from entering.

Slowly, Jennings removed her hand from the window handle. "Then we can't open any of the windows or gunports to fight!"

"You got it, toots."

From the look on her face, George would pay for that "toots" line later. If we lived. And it was becoming a doubtful proposition. The Scion wanted us seriously dead. Or more correctly, they wanted us dead and to get their claws on all the information we carried on the Bureau and its operations. Our organization was the only real deterrent they had ever faced.

"Ed, what do we do?" asked Raul in concern. Hindered by the sheet of unbreakable glass between ourselves and the Scion, even magic was under severe limitations.

Donaher released a flood of oil from the bottom of the van, followed by a rain of nail-clusters. There was no appreciable effect on the Scion.

"First, we're doing a Clean Sweep," I announced. Removing the cigarette lighter, I shoved a finger into the hole where no sane person would shove a finger. As my prints were identified, a small panel swung out from the dashboard and I hastily typed in a Go code. The tiny computer screen repeated a request for authorization, asked several secret questions and when finally satisfied, gave a good long beep.

With a sigh, I reclined in my seat. There: every computer file in the van was deleted and being overwritten with the collected works of Oscar Wilde, my favorite author. Afterwards, the disks would be deleted again, melted, and then diced to pieces. Go ahead and try to reconstruct those records, ya bozos.

Brutally, our vehicle was pounded under a hail of armor-piercing bullets—which didn't. Score another win for TechServ.

In less than a minute, the rest of the team had perfomed similar procedures on their own private records, and Jessica had armed the self-destruct on the van. With six hundred pounds of thermite packed into the hull, the werewolves might capture our dead bodies, but not in large enough pieces to even make a zombie hors d'oeuvre. The Scion was getting nothing from us. Period. End of discussion.

A rocket streaked by, taking the side-view mirror. Uh-oh, they were in trouble now. That's seven years' bad luck.

"What next, Ed?" asked Father Donaher, crumbling a sheet of ashed paper into a nonreconstructible mess.

More bullets. Banged off the windows.

"We'll use the lasers," I declared, holstering my Magnums.

Smiling, Renault fumbled at the vault in our arsenal and withdrew four sleek pistols. Top-secret weapons built for the Pentagon, the futuristic power pistols delivered the punch of an angry lightning bolt, but occasionally exploded on the user and took a week to recharge. We saved them for dire emergencies only.

Dutifully, we switched the pistols' setting from Flash, a disabling light burst that would temporarily blind anyone not wearing polarized goggles, to Beam, a polycyclic ray that cut steel. When we play, we play for keeps.

Crowding to the extreme right side of the van, Donaher, Renault, Mindy and I braced our pistols in our hands while, on the other side, Raul and Tina copied our position with their wands. They had a Deadly Light spell very similar to what our pistols could produce. And with the same limitations. The only real difference between technology and magic was who held the patent: GE or God.

The motorcycles came closer. A LAW struck just aft of us, clouding our view with flame and hunks of concrete. A chance chunk of shrapnel hit the rear Armorlite window and a small crack appeared.

"On my mark," I commanded with a dry mouth. "Ready . . . aim . . . fire!"

And straight through the clear-glass rear windows of the van there lanced out half a dozen scintillating energy beams. Only a fleeting touch of each beam was necessary for the werewolf rider to fall, minus a head or arm. Systematically, we cleared the road. But as the charred bodies dropped lifeless to the highway surface and bounced away, the motorcycles leapt forward with renewed speed.

"Tricked!" cried Donaher, slamming a fist onto a knee. "The motorcycles are the attackers, not the drivers!"

Mindy brushed a strand of sweaty hair off her face. The temperature of the RV must have risen twenty degrees from the secondary effect of the lasers. "Got to be demonically possessed," she swore.

"Ah, not necessarily," said Raul with a pained expression.

Oh, what now?

"Report," I ordered, annoyed. The power level on my laser read 50 percent.

Tina started studying the ceiling, and Raul cleared his throat. "Well, there is this theory. Only a theory, mind you—"

"Talk!" yelled Renault impatiently.

A sigh. "It is believed by some wizards that if werewolves were to become sentient, they could decide what the curse would change the victim into."

Silence filled the van for a small eternity.

"Anything?" gulped Mindy.

A solemn nod.

"So those might not be from the Scion, but—"

"Scion members themselves. Correct."

Intelligent, hostile, paranormal werecycles. Should we lodge a complaint with the Harley-Davidson company or the ASPCA?

"Here they come!"

In a whining roar, the motorcycles surged ahead and we fired again. But this time, the nimble bikes wheeled crazily about in a Gordian knot of confusion, making it impossible for us to get a clear sustained shot. Switching tactics, I ordered the highway destroyed in an effort to make the cycles crash. The lasers brutalized the highway before they winked out. But the sleek two-wheelers merely bounced over the buckled ridges of asphalt. Some of them wobbled badly and almost toppled to the rushing road surface, but then miraculously righted themselves.

Shocked noises filled the van. The damn things must have gyroscope stabilizers! They couldn't fall over!

As the rest of the team heaped verbal abuse on the Scion, a dozen plans went through my mind, each critically flawed by the fact that we still couldn't open the windows because of the nerve gas still adhered to the RV.

Painfully, I gnashed my teeth in frustration. Missiles gone. Out of bullets. Lasers drained. Low on magic. No help was coming. Yet, if we didn't do something fast, those kamikaze kooks would soon reduce us into covert federal hamburger. Desperately, I tried to think of something clever. And succeeded.

"Tina, prepare to cast a Hook. Raul, ready a mass Meld. Mindy, get a stick and some rope from storage. George, grab a map. And everybody get ready to go EVA!"

Nobody bothered to reply. They just did it.

Mindy gave the stick to Jess, who shoved it in between the gas pedal and the dashboard, holding the pedal to the floor. Using the rope, she tied the steering wheel into position.

"Tina? Raul?" I asked, filling my pockets with ammunition and grenades. Just in case this didn't work.

The wizards nodded.

"Hook!" I ordered.

Blanco gestured, and from the side of the van there shot a glowing green chain appended with a giant anchor. It hit the highway and dug in. On screeching tires, the RV brutally arced about on the ethereal tether.

This had to be done perfectly. "Release!"

And the chain was gone. Now facing in the wrong direction, the huge RV hurtled itself towards the enemy bikes.

"Meld!"

Suddenly, we became insubstantial, and moved swiftly through the physical mass of the Bureau vehicle. Standing re-formed on the highway, we watched our twenty-four tons of armored RV race straight at the oncoming array of motorcycles: a solid wall of Detroit metal moving at a relative velocity of 300-plus miles per hour.

Without a doubt, ramming speed.

The whole world seemed to shatter into pieces and then re-form, so powerful was the mass detonation of the motorcycle's explosive cargo of plastique, aided and abetted by the six hundred kilos of thermite in our RV. Shrapnel and bits of concrete pounded all around us, while a brutal shock wave rattled the bones loose in our bodies, a single heartbeat before a boiling thunderhead of flame extended hungrily for us.

"Berlin!" called Tina, and we crouched low behind her magical wall.

Fire engulfed our position, but the licking flames spread out harmlessly as they rebounded from the resilient spell. However, killing heat seeped around the edges and our roasting seemed to last forever.

Eventually, the wall flickered into nothingness as Tina ran dry of magic, and we lay panting in the middle of the disfigured Ohio highway. Battered, broiled, and bone-weary, the team grimly prepared what weapons we had and crossed fingers in a primitive luck ceremony. Failure? Success?

—and from the rumbling fire storm down the road, there appeared a smoking motorcycle tire that rolled aimlessly along for a few meters and then wandered off the road to collapse in the weeds.

We cheered until our throats got as sore as the rest of our bodies. When everybody else is dead, you win: Bureau 13 axiom 7, I do believe.

Romping in from the fiery horizon came Amigo. As he reached our group, the collar around his neck rippled with light, and he was a tiny Gila lizard again.

Picking up our pet, Raul scratched him under the neck and Amigo came as close to a purr as he could.

"Map," I wheezed, loosening my smoking necktie.

Bleeding from both ears, Renault offered the charred piece of paper to me with a bow. I thanked him and managed to focus my vision long enough to see a mile marker and locate our position. Painfully, my team hobbled off the road and headed for the nearest cabstand. We had a lot of work to do, and not much time to do it in. This made twice the Scion had forced us into a retreat.

There would be no third time.

7

As we stumbled into Iron City, our appearance frightened a small child, so we stopped at the local mall and got shaves and haircuts, bought new clothes and wrapped ourselves around a reasonably priced meal at a nice restaurant.

While the team was devouring dessert, I ambled over to a pay phone and placed a discreet call to the Bureau. With the relay in our van gone, our wristwatches probably couldn't reach wherever the heck our HQ was. So the public phone was my sole option. After being endlessly relayed through exchanges in Alamogordo, New Mexico, to Trevose, Pennsylvania, I finally reached somebody in authority I could formally report to. The exchange of information was short and succinct.

Returning to the table, I gleefully informed the group that since we had been in direct telepathic communication with the Scion, no other Bureau team was going to interfere and chance exposure. We alone had been given the honor of stopping the Scion. Somehow, my friends were able to restrain themselves from doing the dance of joy at this news.

Straddling my chair, I called for a group discussion, Tina used a bracelet to cast a small Dome of Silence over the table and everybody gathered in close.

"Okay, obviously we can't go to Hadleyville without some sort of psionic protection," noted George, mopping the last vestiges of gravy from his plate with a buttermilk biscuit. "Raul? Tina? How about some big juju magic?"

Conferring for a moment, the two wizards were glum.

Blanco sighed. "*Nyet*. Spells for minds must be cast on each person, and only last few minutes. Drain Raul and me in quick time."

"Raul and I," corrected Jessica.

A nod. "*Da*, both of us."

Almost knocking over the condiment tray, Horta was madly flipping through his big book of spells, currently disguised as a menu. "There are some alchemical potions which might work, but the side effects are unpleasant," Raul cautioned.

"Such as?" I asked curiously. Headaches? Stomach cramps? We could take those if it got the job done.

Scowling, Raul ran a finger down a page in his book. "Let's see, there is Lungfire, Demonic Cancer, Brain Spiders . . ."

"Enough!" called Mindy, holding up a palm. "We get the general idea."

"And we're eating," munched Renault. There were priorities.

Her steel wand pulsating with flashes of hot power, Tina barked a long phrase in Russian. It didn't sound very cheery.

"This is intolerable!" raged Father Donaher, snapping a bread stick in half easy as a baseball bat. "Just because the Bureau has no operating telepaths, we're supposed to sit on our butts while the Scion does . . ." He gestured vaguely. "Who knows what! How many civilians have died already? And how many more will die?"

It was a good point. Where the Scion went, death followed. And lots of it.

Mindy struck the table a resounding blow with her fist, rattling the silver. "Goddammit! We discover a coven of sentient werewolves, the biggest threat to the world in recent memory, and we can't even *investigate* just because the bad guys can read our minds? I say we go back to Hadleyville anyway, and kick some butt!"

"Yeah!" agreed Raul. "If we move fast enough, or independently, even if they know what we're doing, they may not be able to stop us."

Tina brandished her invisible wand. "We shall bury them!"

"No," I stated in a tone that brooked no further discussion. "The danger is too great. Lord knows what important secrets those Swiftian yahoos have already learned about the Bureau! Jessica saved our hides before, and we're not going to muck up the mission now by charging in unprepared. We'll find a way to stop the Scion. A trick, a trap!"

Everybody looked at me expectantly.

"Something," I mumbled lamely.

"We always do," added Jess, trying to be helpful.

Reclining contentedly in his swivel chair, Horta crossed his arms. "Okay, then shoot us the straight poop, boss man."

Furrowing my brow, I revved my brain to overload and thought like a sonofabitch. No . . . no . . . nyah, that wouldn't work either . . . ah . . . er . . . um . . .

Silent during the rhetoric, Father Donaher sat hunched over, doing his rosary at record speed and starting to break into a sweat. Then he stopped, crossed himself and wet his lip.

"Yes," said Mike in a strained voice as he stared at the ceiling fan overhead. "If only we knew of some . . . thing that could help us. But say, if some priest had heard of such a . . . thing in, oh, the confessional, for example, then he couldn't tell anybody about it.

"Even if he really, really wanted to," finished the big priest with a pained expression.

Smiles abounded. We have a bingo.

"Hey, Mike." I grinned at him. "How about we go stretch our legs in the parking lot outside and maybe have a friendly game of darts?"

Tongue between teeth, Raul was already digging about in his spell book and extricated a giant map of North America. We had done this before. Many times.

Pulling a brass-trimmed, red leather box from a voluminous pocket of his cassock, Donaher eased open the top. Lying inside on a cushion of gleaming white satin were three darts. The needle tips were engraved with Donaher's full name, the shaft made of African ironwood, edged with mahogany, and the fletching was of the neatly trimmed feathers of an American bald eagle.

Daintily lifting a dart into view, Donaher flipped it into the air and on the way down caught the point between thumb and forefinger. Mike flipped it again and caught the dart underhand with a snapping wrist motion. Mindy couldn't have done better.

"Gosh, Ed," said the priest. "I'll be glad to play a game, but I'm really not as good at darts as I would like to be."

The two of us played darts across four states before we "needed" a fresh map to replace the old one. Pretty soon, Mike and I were working on a street map of Kansas City, Missouri. In amazing accuracy he laid a feathered pattern in the suburbs around a small estate owned by an old friend of ours. That is, if you use some new and twisted meaning of the word "friend."

Gathering the crew, we paid for dinner and took a cab from Iron City to Zanesville, sleeping the whole way. In Zanesville, we purchased a brand-new limousine using my disposable ID and fake American Express card listed under the name of Hank Mathers. The credit card was good for any amount, but only for one purchase. Afterwards, the account would be paid in full by the Bureau and permanently closed.

Driving to Columbus, we traded the limo in for a used school bus, which was the closet thing to an armored assault vehicle it was possible to obtain on such short notice. It also helped to muddy our trail in case the Scion was still after us. Not an unreasonable assumption. Those guys could give bloodhounds a bad name.

Hitting a theatrical supply company, we purchased the few additional supplies needed to do this assignment and then took off to find some secluded place where we could work in peace.

Pulling into the lot of the Lazy Eight Motel, Jessica got us four adjoining rooms, and the team trundled inside with our new equipment. Most of it was weapons, ammunition, medical supplies, silver ingots and a special purchase by me, for me. I might have no idea what Donaher was sending us after, but I had a pretty good hunch what I would have to do to get it.

As this mission was incredibly dangerous, and slightly illegal, I was going alone. The more people involved, the bigger a chance of failure. It was not a unanimous choice, and, in fact, I had to pull executive privilege, something I had not done since that nasty Colombian incident with the New Gods. But we knew who that suburban mansion belonged to.

Dr. Mathais Bolt was a medical doctor, licensed psychotherapist, millionaire, philanthropist, wizard, necromancer, murderer and leader of the Brotherhood of Darkness, a lunatic cult dedicated to conquering the world. Probably so the losers could get dates for Saturday night, and avoid paying taxes. Who knew?

The Brotherhood of Darkness had never been a serious threat to the Bureau, or the world in general, even though Dr. Mathais Bolt was the best . . . er, make that the most powerful, necromancer in the world. On the other hand, some of the members of the Brotherhood were smart. Too smart. So the only way to handle them was to give the loonies all the information they could handle, but make them believe that it was totally false. Reverse psychology was what the gang in Strategy & Tactical called it. Field agents called the process "polishing the mirror."

Stripping naked, I hit the shower, scrubbed myself painfully clean and dressed in brand-new clothes. Then I carefully dyed my black hair the color black. Next, I smoothed a clear suntan lotion on my normally dusky hands and face. I slid on a padded corset and slipped on shoes with hollow heels twice the thickness of regular shoe heels. Clear, nonmagnifying contact lenses went into both eyes, and lastly, I removed my wedding ring, used a tanning cream to overcolor the pale band on my finger, then placed the ring back on.

Carefully, I scrutinized myself from head to toe. Perfect!

To a casual observer, I appeared as always. But to a trained observer, I was obviously in disguise. My hair color had none of the minor color differences of natural hair. Obviously, it was dyed. The same with skin tone. I was wearing contacts, so black was not my natural eye color, and I had an old scratched wedding ring with no pale-skin band underneath. Plainly false. Shoe lifts meant I was short. And the padded corset indicated I was fatter than appeared and was trying to hide the weight.

Plus, I had a bulky Smith & Wesson .357 Magnum in a shoulder holster built for a slim automatic pistol. Nobody would switch holsters, so a Magnum was obviously not my standard gun.

I had just successfully polished the mirror. I looked exactly like myself, only nobody would believe it. No fool, that is. Which is what I was counting on.

I padded to the main bedroom, where the gang was waiting for me. Raul was chanting over a coffeepot filled with a foul-smelling brew, and Jessica was loading a hypodermic syringe.

Tossing my necktie over a shoulder, I unbuttoned my shirt and lifted my body armor. Soft as silk, the stuff would stop anything this side of an elephant gun.

"This may hurt," said Jess, wiping my amazingly muscular torso with an alcohol swap.

"Do I get a lollipop afterwards?" I asked.

Gently, Jessica impaled me. Ouch! "Sure. If you don't cry."

Tried my best not to. Whew. Who makes those things? Nazi war criminals? Then my skin went numb as the novocaine took effect. Ah, much better.

Jess stepped aside, and Tina moved in to sketch a diagram on my chest. Kind of tickled. Then Raul took her place, and with a brush painted over the outline. Even through the novocaine, I could feel the occult brew sizzling into my tender skin. Goodbye, summer tan.

"Is this going to leave a scar?" I demanded when he finally allowed me to lower my body armor.

"Gosh, I hope so," he said, pouring the rest of the concoction into the sink. The enamel began to peel off.

I stopped my buttoning. "What! Why?"

"It'll last longer," smirked Raul, tossing the brush into a waste can. A piece of old newspaper flared into ash.

Swell. "Thank you, Mr. Wizard."

Horta did a sweeping bow. "At your service, sahib."

After checking the load on my Magnum, I bowed my head as Father Donaher did a little prayer over me, lifted a pants leg as George strapped on an ankle holster and accepted a fistful of pens from Mindy. She had personally filled and primed each, thereby greatly reducing the chance of a dysfunction. Tina poured some powders into my shoes, a potion in my mouth and a lotion down my back. My chest burned, my head ached and I was starting to feel a bit slimy. Yuck. The things I do for America.

Then Jess gave me a glass of water and some extra-strength aspirin. God, I love that woman.

After issuing some detailed instructions to the gang and receiving a priority kiss from Jess, I went outside, hailed a cab, went downtown, bought another car and boldly drove to the known headquarters of our archenemies.

Briefly, I again wondered what it was that Donaher thought was so damn important.

Strategically, I parked my car a good block away from the mansion, stopping directly under an old oak tree whose spreading branches offered a pool of shadows from the overhead streetlamps. Every little bit helps.

Dominating the street was a brilliantly illuminated billboard announcing that this was the headquarters of the Brotherhood, a nonprofit, charitable organization and equal opportunity employer.

Openly, the Brotherhood was a publicly chartered organization dedicated to the study of magic, parapsychology and the occult science. Their agents provocateurs never went anywhere without a lawyer, which made for interesting firefights. They actively sought the company of news reporters and protected themselves with the continued association of innocent civilians. A dirty trick that worked much too well.

Their Kansas City base shared land with a unique orphanage for the blind and a training center for the physically handicapped. Both of these noteworthy institutions were supported by the blood money of the Brotherhood. Totally unconcerned with the welfare of these trusting people, the Brotherhood looked upon them merely as protective coverage. The Bureau couldn't simply, say, drop a plane full of napalm upon the mansion, as these sister organizations would also be destroyed. And the matter had been discussed. In detail.

The Brotherhood of Darkness was sneaky, tricky and damn annoying. They used our own laws against us. If I tried to strong-arm my way in, a horde of lawyers wearing pin-striped polyester would descend, each loudly demanding to see my search warrant, holding order, writ of habeas corpus, FBI badge, driver's license, fishing license, birth certificate and anything else they could think of. If trouble occurred, a TV news team would be there within minutes.

Therefore, I couldn't bluff my way in. I couldn't use force. And with all of their magical and technological defensives, I couldn't sneak inside. That left only one remaining option, the most dangerous and difficult of all:

Knocking on the front door and asking for admittance.

Strolling across the street, I noted that the fence was made of brick and about six feet tall. Which was exactly as high as the law allowed. But topping the brick were shiny swirls of concertina wire. Hardly more than an endless razor blade, concertina wire would slice through leather gloves, and the hands inside, with frightening ease.

Halogen light clusters—which are very difficult to shoot out—dotted the double fence every eight meters. There was only one gate, stainless steel painted a nondescript black. There were no hinges. The massive two-ton slab of metal lowered and raised from the concrete apron of the driveway, lifted by a set of hydraulic motors big enough to lift the fence, not to mention the gate.

Of course, there were guards.

Standing in a cute little brick gatehouse, whose inner walls were plated with Soviet Army reactive armor, were a man and woman in baggy uniforms designed to hide the body armor underneath. Openly, the pair carried Ruger .38 service revolvers. Legal, if kind of wimpy. But in the arms locker of the gatehouse was a nasty assortment of military deathdealers, and a large cache of thermite bombs powerful enough to fry God.

As I came close, the woman started talking into a hand radio, video cameras swung my way and the man rested his thumbs in his belt so that his hands were closer to his pistol.

"Good evening," I said politely, offering my hand.

Hesitantly, he took it and we shook. The goof.

"Sir," he replied stiffly.

"I would like to see Dr. Bolt, please. Is he in?"

"Do you have an appointment?" asked the man, reclaiming his hand. Too late!

"No."

"Then I am sorry, sir, but Dr. Bolt is a very busy man," apologized the guard. "Perhaps if you called his secretary in the morning for an appointment?"

Hell would freeze first, bucko.

"I'm afraid the matter cannot wait," I said amiably.

The woman was on the radio again.

"And you are, sir?" asked the man.

Casually, I reached inside my sports jacket and withdrew an amazingly clean FBI commission booklet. The badge was real and the card showed my picture. But there the identity process ended.

"Special Agent Emmanuel Rodriguez," I stated. "Federal Bureau of Investigation."

The guards grew more attentive. The Brotherhood could not know for certain, but I was sure they harbored notions who the Bureau was a subdivision of.

"And exactly what is your business with Dr. Bolt?" asked the woman, speaking for the first time.

"Private," I said, letting the cold ring of authority enter my voice.

Stepping close together, they held a private conversation, so I gazed at the stars overhead. Such a beautiful night. What was the chance of a meteor hitting this place? Sadly, none at all.

"If you would just wait a moment, Officer?" said the man as the woman stepped into the gatehouse and started dialing the phone.

Nodding, I slid my commission booklet into my breast pocket so that the shiny badge was always visible. "Of course."

Privately, I hoped somebody got rude real soon. This artificial smiling was starting to make my jaw hurt.

In less than a minute, four more guards appeared on the other side of the fence, and I was informed that Dr. Bolt would be delighted to see me. Anything to assist the authorities.

The gates opened with the sound of a bank vault, and if the new guards didn't quite frog-march me across the lawn, they sure came close. Naturally, I didn't get much chance to view the external grounds, but that wasn't important. I had already seen the aerial photos in the Bureau file room. Mostly, it was plush lawns, manicured hedges and splashing fountains. But lining the broad front walk was a double row of bronze statues depicting the signs of the zodiac: Aries the ram, Taurus the bull, the Gemini twins, Cancer the crab, Leo the lion, a nude woman for Virgo, a dressed woman holding a pair of scales for Libra, a scorpion for Scorpio, a nude man with a quiver and bow for Sagittarius, Capricorn the goat, a scantily dressed woman pouring water from a jug for Aquarius and this really big fish for Pisces.

I'm not much of an art buff, but they were beautiful sculptures. And it didn't take much surmise on my part to guess that in case of trouble the whole damn zodiac would come to life and the horrorscope of any invader would read "Time to die, bozo." Nuff said.

The front doors were made of aged seasoned oak, thick enough to stop a medieval battering ram. And while I wasn't wearing my sunglasses, somehow I could still tell that the butler was a zombie. Or else truly British. Sometimes the distinction is difficult to make. I offered my hand, and he gave it the most perfunctory of clasps. Ha! Got you!

The foyer was Italian marble, a French crystal chandelier filled the ceiling overhead and suits of old German armor stood at rigid attention in recessed niches in the wall. I was starting to get the idea that Bolt was more paranoid than the Bureau. Did we actually rag his case this much, a pleasant notion, or did he have more enemies than just the Bureau, an even more pleasing idea? Hmm.

The guards stayed at attention in the foyer, and I shook

their hands goodbye, then tagged along after the icy butler. At the top of the stairs, more guards were waiting and we shook hello. I am such a friendly guy. Then we formed a procession down a hallway full of locked doors and portraits whose beady eyes followed every move I made. Faintly, I heard the telltale noise of a machine-gun bolt being pulled. Maybe this hadn't been such a great idea. Below, on the ground floor, the great front door boomed shut with the noise of a coffin lid closing.

Eek! Symbolism.

8

As we strolled merrily along the corridor, the guards managed to accidentally-on-purpose bump into me several times as they attempted to take an inventory of what I carried. A partial inventory anyway. I had more weapons and equipment than these yutzes could ever imagine. I only hoped it was enough.

Turning a corner, we passed through a cleverly disguised X-ray machine and ankled past a hidden machine-gun nest and several infrared scanners. This might be more difficult than previously imagined. And I still didn't know what I was here for!

At the end of the corridor was a simple wooden door marked "office." The four guards took positions outside the room while the butler opened the door and followed me in.

Ah, at last.

Foolishly, I had half expected the private office of Mathais Bolt to resemble a mad scientist's laboratory with bubbling experiments, a dissection table overflowing with blood-stained reports, shelves made of human bones bowing under the weight of forbidden books of alchemy and black magic. Actually, the place was rather nice. A bit conservative for my taste, but not bad.

The walls were lined with bookcases filled with leather-bound volumes in a hundred colors and a dozen languages. The floor was a plush velour carpet which hid my ankles, and so soft it made you want to lie down with your best girl. Almost felt alive. Centering the left wall was a fireplace you could cook a car in, and right was dominated by a Belgian tapestry large enough to hide almost anything.

Over by the far wall, bracketed by a pair of balcony windows, was a massive slab of mahogany pretending to be a desk. The flawless surface was polished mirror bright. The only items displayed were a gilt-edged leather blotter with green paper, and a gold pen and pencil set in a rectangle of white marble. I was sure that all of them were deadly weapons.

Behind the desk, waiting for me, was Mathais Bolt.

His eyes were the very first thing that a person noticed. They were overly large, set deep into his skull, and never blinked. Creepy.

A slim dapper man, Bolt was wearing a velvet smoking jacket and silk lounging pajamas. Geez, who still made those things? If his mouth was too broad for smiling, he did it anyway. Mathais had hair coal black, with streaks of pure silver at each temple. Dr. Bolt was smoking what smelled like an herbal Egyptian cigarette in an ebony Chinese holder a foot long. Although wearing no rings or watch, Necro-Man had a plain band of copper adorning each wrist. Ah, magic bracelets. Same as mine. This could get interesting. Depending upon your definition of the word. Was a nuclear war interesting? In the movies—sure. Live? Well . . .

Puffing on his cigarette, Bolt reminded me of a big snake preparing to eat a small bird. And I was the guy wearing feathers. Briefly, I wondered if he had forged the bands himself or stolen them from the cooling bodies of dead Bureau agents. Either way made him a man to be reckoned with. And disposed of as soon as possible.

For a moment I toyed with the concept of gunning him down on the spot, but dismissed the notion. Not only was it illegal, not to mention bad manners, but he had yet to tell me what I was here for.

That was when I noticed the *Playboy* calendar on the wall. Wow. June was a good month. Maybe the old necromancer was subhuman at that.

Grandly, the leader of the Brotherhood of Darkness gestured towards a plush chair that was so softly cushioned it would be impossible to get out of in a hurry.

Our battle had begun. *En garde!*

I parried by accepting the seat and snuggled in deep. That should put Mathais at ease and put him off guard. Ha! Bureau 13 agents were deadly even if stark naked, upside down and chained to the wall, and that's the way we like it!

No, wait a minute, I hadn't put that quite correctly.

"Good evening, Agent Smythe," said Mathais Bolt in a voice so soothing that I instinctively braced myself against Mind Control.

Then I came fully alert. Smythe? Yikes! A straight lunge to the heart! I hadn't used that name since my old Chicago days as a PI. Did this carrion magician actually know me? No, wait, a whole bunch of bureau people used that now. Whew.

"Who?" I asked with a puzzled expression, dancing aside and keeping my guard raised. "I'm sorry. Your butler got the name wrong. It's Emmanuel Rodriguez, Special Agent, FBI."

"Of course," he purred, oozing charm. "My mistake. I will fire the incompetent bungler immediately."

Slash, and miss.

I covered a yawn as my riposte. Nice try, bozo. But if he was attempting to incur my sympathy and thus weaken my resolve, he had the wrong man. We Smythes are a fighting people.

"So why is the Bureau"—he stressed the word—"gracing me with a visit at ten-thirty at night?" Thrust.

"Official business," I said gruffly, placing my shoes on his desktop and deliberately marring the perfect finish. Parry and lunge.

Dr. Bolt turned red in the face, then puffed himself to quiet complacency. "Indeed? What, pray tell?" Maintain guard, backstep.

Going for the kill, I gave him a death's-head grin, honed from a thousand poker games and specifically designed to freeze the very blood in your veins. Had actually worked once on a naive vampire.

"You ever hear of a Bureau 13?" I countered bluntly.

Astonished, Dr. Bolt dropped his cigarette holder and then yelped as he burnt his foot. First blood!

"Why, ah, yes," he responded, opening a drawer in the

desk and extracting a small manila folder. "I have even been made privy to a file amassed on a quote Bureau 13—"

Whatever information was in that folder bode ill for me. There were a dozen defenses in my repartee, so I chose the classical best. Offense.

From the hum in the bracelet on my left wrist, I could tell that Bolt was protected by a magical forceshield a bazooka shell couldn't get through. But the paper file was on the desk, and tagged with the red edge denoting a non duplicable original.

With the flick of a wrist, I activated the second function of my cigarette lighter and aimed the stream of liquid fire directly toward Dr. Bolt. A burning lance of chemical flame washed over the man, his prismatic shell deflecting the fiery onslaught, but the report flared into ash.

His eyes round as saucers, Bolt lowered his hand and stared at the charred stub of paper.

"Sorry," I said, pocketing the lighter. "These darn things malfunction occasionally."

"Who are you?" he demanded in a very quiet voice.

No more niceties. The game was over. I had openly displayed advanced technology and a knowledge of magic, and his shield spoke volumes about him. We each knew who the other was. Fast, I shook my watch, activating the self-destruct mechanism. A lot depended on what Mathais attacked with next.

"Ask me in Hell," I snarled, placing my feet on the floor and sliding to the edge of the chair. I started to reach for my gun. Horribly, he smiled. As pleasant a sight as a child's grave.

"Accepted," whispered Bolt.

There was no other warning. Exploding across the desk came a boiling wave of intangible force, a hellish tsunami of primordial black magic that blew aside the blotter, exploded the pen and pencils and engulfed me like a blast of live steam.

Frantically, I raised both hands, the copper bracelets tingling as they expended every erg of stored white magic in a desperate counter to the lethal conjure. The very air seemed to seethe as the magiks met and battled it out in silent ethereal combat. Inside my aching skull, my beleaguered brain vibrated under the pounding command to *tell him everything I don't want him to know*!

It was an old spell but a goody.

Then my chest burned as the mystic rune painted there flared in response, absorbing the ethereal onslaught, containing it, controlling it and violently throwing it right back in the face of its caster.

"It's in the desk!" he screamed. I had made him angry enough to try to magically force the truth out of me. And, in return, it had forced the truth out of him.

Panicked, Mathais started to rise and then slowly ground to a halt like an old machine rusting solid. Motionless, hands raised, frozen in the very act of casting some deadly spell.

Aw, too bad, so sad. I win.

With a finger, I toppled him over into his chair and pushed it away from the desk. By necessity, the lotion on my hand that I had used on the staff must act slowly. Otherwise, I wouldn't have been allowed in here. Blasted by his own magic, Bolt was out of commission for nine more minutes, and the item was in the desk. What else did I need? How tough could a desk be?

I soon found out.

Underneath the hutch was a full control panel of hidden buttons, knee switch and foot pedals. Most were labeled, in cryptic symbols of some arcane language that resembled chicken droppings. However, off to one side, behind a sliding panel, was a very modern computer lock keypad. Bingo!

From the burglar's kit in my coat pocket, I dusted the push buttons and found prints on only four of the numbers. Ha! That lowered the math quite a bit. Plus, two of the integers were more worn than the rest. Those had a high probability of the first and last numbers. Start sure and end with a flourish. For all his fault, Mathais Bolt was still a human being. Well, probably.

Unfortunately, there was still a small problem. There was a Stuart Industries box around the keypad.

Originally, electronic boxes had been indelibly stamped

with the name of the manufacturer to help promote sales of the product. But it was soon apparent that this advertising ploy worked against the client. A smart crook would have a library of plans stolen/purchased/copied from each manu-facturer, and after reviewing the schematics of a particular keypad, would simply drill holes in the box at the precise critical points to cut crucial circuits and tremendously ease entry into the home or business.

That is, until Stuart Industries Limited.

Stuart Industries didn't make alarms, security systems or even locks. What they made was boxes. Undecorated, steel-reinforced, dully identical boxes that could hold the works of a hundred other companies. With no brand name to work with, it became a crapshoot for the crooks. Thus, for only a paltry few bucks, a hundred-thousand-dollar security system could be massively augmented.

State prisons were full of master thieves who could attest to the efficiency of the Stuart Box.

Careful not to bump into any of the controls around me, I tapped here and there on the burnished metal cube. Listened, smelled, and glanced at my watch. Five minutes till he broke loose. Think, Alvarez, think! Millionaire bad boy Bolt should have purchased the very best for his private safe. A Gotterstein Deluxe? No, must be a Vische. Okay, go for it.

Holding my breath, I filed a tiny slit in the top of the box exactly seven millimeters from the left side. Uncorking a tiny vial from my kit, I poured in a couple of drops of smelly sulfuric acid, waited ten seconds, eased off the Stuart and tapped in the most likely combination on the keypad.

I allowed myself to inhale again when a section of the desk slid into the floor, exposing a squat armored cube mas-querading as a safe. Turning to smile victoriously at Dr. Bolt, my grin wilted when I saw a barrier of laser beams encir-cling the desk. Extending from ceiling to floor, the beams were barely separated. It would have been difficult to pass a sheet of paper between them. Hoo boy.

Hatefully, Bolt was watching my every move.

Returning to work, I ignored him and the lasers. I still had to breach the safe. Afterwards I'd worry about departing, surviving and secondary stuff like that.

The four dials fronting the safe were in a diamond pattern. Here I was on home turf. It was an Anderson. Two were real, two were armed with explosives, but all joined in the middle where the master support bar of ultra-rigid titanium steel pivoted the semi-flexible sidereal arms of nickel-cobalt to activate the easily melted copper drop pins that retained the eighteen independent dead bolts which held the six-inch-thick alloy door closed. She was a bitch to blow, burn or pick your way into. But I had an answer to that.

Four minutes.

From my kit I withdrew a fat tube and removed the crinkly plastic wrapper. A DeTalion Turbo-Drill. This tool was so new it was not even on the market yet. But I had read about it in *Popular Science* and used my FBI clearance to get one immediately. I was sure they would soon be all the rage among the crooks and brain surgeons.

With a tiny click, the miniature battery started revving the small electric motor. Then the tube jerked as the motor finally obtained operational speed and activated the main flywheel assembly. The soft vibration in the tool increased as the flywheel reached the necessary RPM to activate the main air turbine, and a warm breeze blew on my hand as the turbine whined into the ultrasonic range.

Now rotating at half a million RPM, the carbide-steel drill bit was moving so fast it appeared to be smooth metal. Touching the tip to the alloy of the safe, a fine mist of metal filings sprayed out as I started to carve a path around the dial. Offensive technology had finally caught up with defensive, and the centuries-old technique of a "punch job" had returned to safecracking. Made me proud to be an American.

At the three-minute mark, I finished cutting the desired pattern, the dials spun themselves like crazy and the bolts disengaged. Killing the DeTalion, I placed the warm vibrating tube tenderly in my kit and eased the door open, being wary of any additional magical or demonic defenses. But there was none.

Inside, the safe was stacked with mounds of cash, a clear-plastic box filed with vials of colored liquids and a flat jewelry box. Sliding on my kid-leather beauties, I eased open the case so that it was facing away from me. There was a puff of greenish smoke and a dart thumped into the carpet. Satisfied the booby traps were all deboobied, I rotated the case and looked inside.

I think my eyes left my head. Silently, I sent heartfelt thanks to whoever watched over fools and private dicks. If I hadn't been wearing gloves when I picked up this case, my hat size would now be zero. Because no catalog of legendary occult amulets was necessary for me to recognize the infamous Necklace of Me.

A millenium or so ago, a nameless, and quite mad, master magician who had been born mute forged a unique amulet out of metals stolen from the center of the Earth, smelted in a furnace fed by trees he had personally grown and quenched in a bucket of his own blood. To say that this guy needed a hobby was putting it mildly.

With this necklace, whenever the mage thought of a person he disliked, the poor slob would be bodily torn to pieces by the thundering clarion telepath call of *"It's me!"* Hence the name.

Although weakened by the passage of thousands of years, it was still a lethal psionic booster. Now without a master, Me wildly amplified the telepathic ability inherent in any person, so that with a single touch your head would explode. Nobody could touch the amulet and live. Nobody with even the faintest smidgen of telepathic powers.

Except, perhaps, for my telepathically dead wife.

Wrapping the case in a Bureau handkerchief, I slid it into an inside pocket of my jacket and buttoned the flap down. After what I went through to get Me, I was taking no chances on losing it.

Job done. Two minutes remaining. In smirking satisfaction, the impulse came upon me to take the money. Or burn it. Depriving the Brotherhood of a few million in cash would seriously hinder their operations.

Unfortunately, the vials of chemicals and the cash were the undeniably legitimate property of the Brotherhood. Sad,

but true, and as a cop I had to draw the line somewhere. I
know that George would have no such reticence. Or Mindy,
for that matter. Which is why neither would ever lead their
own field team. But I did. Ah well, sometimes it was tough
being the good guy.

However, this necklace was stolen property. Not provable
in court, but the truth nonetheless. I felt little remorse reclaiming the dangerous artifact from homicidal lunatics.

Duck-walking out from under the desk, I stood with a
creak. Standing inches away from the wall of laser beams, I
could truly appreciate their searing gigawatt majesty. With a
flick of my right wrist, I activated my next to last magic
bracelet and turned invisible. Unharmed, I stepped through
the deadly curtain of lasing photons. With no colors to react
to, a laser is just so much indirect lighting. Ain't science
grand?

But at the exact moment the jewelry case passed the brink
of the lasers, I heard glass shatter. Eh? Pivoting, I saw the
broken vials in the safe, their bubbling liquid contents comb-
ining into a translucent greenish ooze, which broke apart
into small spheres and bounced to the floor. Pulsating, they
commenced to grow: Ping-Pong balls, baseballs, basket-
balls . . .

Utilizing extreme wisdom, I ran for my frigging life.

In the hallway, I nearly tripped over the sleeping guards to
whom I had given the ol' Morpheus happy handshake. I
made it past the infrared sensors no problem, and passed
through the X-rays as easily as they did me. But I paused at
the top of the main staircase. The winding expanse of carpeted marble steps appeared totally innocent, open and safe.

In this place? Yeah, right. Now sell me some swampland
only driven by a little old lady minister on Sundays.

Removing a special Bureau device from my side pocket, I
placed it at the top of the stairs and with a finger push started
the Slinky down the steps.

Ka-ching, ka-ching. Arrows flew, bullets zinged, flame
whooshed, poison gas hissed, spears jabbed, swinging
blades did, crashing weights also. But at knee and chest

level. Casually, I strolled along in the calm wake behind my diminutive six-inch-tall assistant. *Ka-ching, ka-ching.*

At the bottom landing I reclaimed the oiled coil and was forced to nudge the snoring butler out of the way of the front door. The empty suits of armor stirred at the action but did not attack.

Stepping outside, I closed the door as quietly as possible. Safe! The Brotherhood mansion was tightly sealed against teleporting and Gating. But once off the front veranda, I was home free! A bronze arrow the size of a javelin slammed into the door frame. Turning, I saw the whole zodiac advancing towards me. Oops.

Nimbly, I ducked between the shapely legs of Virgo and outmaneuvered the Gemini twins, the hollow metal giants clanging like church bells when they collided, but Aquarius drowned me in water and Leo pinned me to the ground under paws the size of sofas. Shaking the fluid from my ears, I could hear sirens starting to wail, and yawning guards were stumbling onto the grounds. Options came and went in my mind like the fluttering pages of a book. I was only a yard from freedom. But my Magnums, grenades, acid-squirting pen, pocketknife, dazzling personality, nothing I had could even dent those bronze Titans.

No. Wait. That was wrong.

Taking the jewelry case from my coat, I tore off the handkerchief and tossed it at the lion. Leo made the catch in his mouth . . . and his head exploded.

Moving fast, Virgo snatched the case before it hit the ground, and her skull went blooey. Pisces made a successful snap and got psionic lobotomy.

Animating inanimate objects was always a tricky job. Being born dead, they were incredibly stupid and your instructions had to be most explicit. Bolt had probably ordered them to get the necklace.

Well, they got it. Each and every one.

Bullets were starting to fly my way while I used gloves and handkerchief to recover the jewelry case from amid the jumble of headless bronze junk. Contemptuously, I thumbed my nose at the onrushing guards in the official Bureau 13 sa-

lute to bad guys, took two giant steps and used my last bracelet to teleport away.

As per regulations, I appeared in the parking lot of the motel
instead of our rooms. That was just in case anything could
follow a teleport. Ha. What a laugh.

Then a swarm of demonic black balls appeared.

Yikes! God bless regulations.

Cursing Mathais Bolt, I emptied my pistols at the bouncing spheres. I raced across the parking lot and hit the door to
our room in a baseball tackle worthy of any center. The
cheap wood bent alarmingly under my strike, but held, then
the lock popped and I lunged into what I sincerely hoped
was the correct room.

"Orson Welles!" I cried, announcing the invasion and diving over the bed towards my suitcase.

My team turned, and the balls were upon us.

Closest to the door, George dropped his sandwich and
kicked over the television on top of the first globe. In an explosion of electrical sparks, the black thing was gone.

Spinning around from the sink, Jessica quick-drew her
Uzi and started pumping 9mm rounds into the demonic . . .
whatever these things were. Satan's beach balls?

Larger than the rest, King Beach Ball hissed a billowing
cloud which set fire to a cushioned chair, while another
spewed a stream of brackish liquid at me. Fast as possible, I
ducked out of the way, and the vicious liquid hit the wall, dissolving the wood panels, glass mirror and lamp. Wow. Talk
about morning breath.

Slamming a clip into an Uzi machine pistol, I gave the
devil rounders a taste of 9mm Parabellums a la Alvarez.

Charging in from the parking lot came two more beach
balls. Frantically, Raul gestured and a loud grinding noise
came from the doorway, although nothing was visible. Unstoppable, the balls leapt into the air to sail through the doorway at us.

Bad move. As the globes crossed the doorjamb and hit the
portal of Wering, they were converted into a fine mist which

sprayed across the hotel room, dampening the carpet and wetting the bed.

However, our bullets were not doing so well. Lead slugs simply bounced off their adamantine hides, phosphorous rounds flattened as glowing dots of yellow fire, the steel rounds musically ricocheted away and blessed wood splintered. Ah, but then I noticed that silver bullets hit the beach balls with sledgehammer force. Ah-hah! I tried to keep them busy while Jess got more silver ammunition.

Going for her sword, Mindy flipped over backwards in her chair as a ball jumped to get her. As it passed overhead, a slim hand holding a silver knife shot up and gutted the thing in midflight. Deflated, it collapsed and vanished.

Just then the bathroom door was shoved aside and out came Christina Balnco, stark naked, dripping wet, hair matted with shampoo and the four feet of stainless-steel wizard's wand held in both hands. As lovely as the lady is, I was more pleased to see the staff than her ample feminine charms.

" . . . !" shouted the woman, her staff pointed at one of the monsters. It went motionless and turned gray as stone.

Bouncing off a wall, a particularly nimble beach ball went careening towards Father Donaher. Swinging, he slapped the thing in the head with his steel-reinforced Bible. There was an audible crunch, and the black globe dropped to the carpeted floor incredibly dead.

"Get thee back, hellspawn!" bellowed the big priest, the golden cross in his hand ablaze with holy power. Snarls of rage from the globes changed into whimpers of fear and the demonic balls retreated.

Snapping the bolt and clicking off the safety, George added the firepower of the big M-60 to the battle, spraying a glittering stream of silver rounds into the remaining demons trapped between the intoning priest and the doorway jammed full of an invisible lawn mower. Steadily blown to pieces, the scraps started to roll into tiny spheres, which began pulsating and growing again.

Inspiration! Maintaining fire with the Uzi, I dug inside my pocket and tossed the jewelry case towards my wife. My shirt had ridden up in the battle and the box nudged my bare wrist. Fleeting as the touch was, my entire left arm went limp and I was blinded by the mother of headaches.

Through tears of pain, I saw Jess make the catch one-handed, but then stagger violently backwards against the wall, her small body rigid in pain.

Oh no.

9

Instantly, my wife recovered, her eyes narrowing in concentration. Standing straight, Jessica turned towards the bouncing demons totally confident. Yowsa! I hadn't seen her like this in years.

"Die!" she growled, clutching the necklace in her bare hands.

Both of the remaining creatures went stock-still and tiny wisps of steam rose from the bits scattered about on the floor. Equally exhausted, I slumped to the floor.

Dumbfounded, my team stared with slack jaws.

"How the hell . . . ?"

"But that's impossible . . ."

"Could it be . . . ?"

Raul spun about. "When the bloody heck did you get your telepathic powers back?"

Just now, she sent softly, fingering the glowing necklace in her hands.

"Happy birthday," I groaned from behind the ruin of the bed.

They rushed forward and helped me to my feet.

No pain, sent Jess.

My head pieced itself together. *Gracias, hon.*

You're welcome, pumpkin.

Sssh!

Sheathing her sword, Mindy helped me into a chair while Raul gave me a bottle of Healing potion and George offered a beer. As I thanked each of them, I gazed hard into the faces of my teammates. Okay, apparently nobody had received the "P" word. My pride was yet intact.

"Report," ordered Father Donaher in a good impression of me.

I took a healthy swig from the Healing potion and my aches went away. Then I took a swallow from the beer and my thirst went away. Alternating sips from the two bottles, I gave the pertinent details: Mathais, rune, safe, statues, balls.

Sitting boneless in a chair, his feet dangling, Raul massaged his chin. "So the brotherhood can track a 'port. I'll have to do some work on that."

"Definitely," I agreed.

Tina jerked her head. "Raul!" she screamed, pointing.

Weapons at the ready, we turned to see the angry manager of the motel stepping through the doorway. Horta gestured so hard and fast to cancel the earlier spell, he fell out of his chair, but the man stayed in one piece as he walked into the room. Whew, that was close.

"What the hell is going on here!" stormed the manager. His name tag said, "Fred," and the bulge over his belt said "diet."

Moving fast, Jessica took his head in her hands and his eyes glazed over.

"We're a famous rock band," she said aloud to reinforce the hypnotic illusion. "We're here in disguise to escape our fans. We have given you a deposit of five—"

Donaher lifted a pack of cash from our emergency stash.

". . . ten thousand dollars for any damages we might incur to your property. You interrupted us in the middle of an orgy. You joined in for a while, and now, totally sated, you're going back to the office for a nap."

She released his head.

"Take care, gang," he said with a wave, and ambled away. Whistling a Beatles tune? Hey, get MTV, pal!

Chuckling, I locked the door, Raul closed the window curtains and George offered Tina a robe. She looked puzzled, then laughed.

"*Da!* Nudity taboo. Forget. I go finish shower."

Unconcerned, the natural blonde strolled into the bathroom and soon the sound of running water was heard again.

"Conference," I announced, pulling up a chair.

"Wait," Jessica commanded, and slowly revolved once, twice.

"There." She sighed and smiled. "I've put everybody in the motel asleep again and sent the police off to the nearest doughnut shop."

Will that accursed stereotype never die?

Meanwhile, the rest of the team had gathered cushions and chairs around me to form a rough circle. That way we could talk face-to-face and watch each other's back.

"Okay. We have protection again," I started, resting my arms on my knees. "What's the fastest way to get a replacement Bureau vehicle, so that we can go and crack this Hadleyville nut?"

"The more time the Scion is left unsupervised, the harder it will be to stop them," agreed Renault.

"Closest supply dump is our own in Chicago," stated Mindy, sitting cross-legged on the rumpled bed. "With Raul and Tina too drained for a mass teleport or Gate, it'll take us five, six hours to drive there."

"Only two if we put Flash Renault behind the wheel," gibed Father Donaher.

Sucking on a fresh lollipop, George was not insulted. Our daredevil firmly believed that highway speed limits were merely social guidelines to be used by the weak and confused.

"We could ask for an airdrop," suggested Horta.

"Air-drop an RV?" Jess gave a snort.

"Okay," relented the wizard. "How about a nice tank?"

"Might as well announce ourselves to the media with a bullhorn."

"Hrmph," he grumped.

"Then again, maybe we don't need an armored assault vehicle," I said half to myself.

That caught their attention.

"Whatcha mean, Ed?" queried Raul.

"The Scion might think that we died on the Ohio highway," I explained. "If so, we can sneak back, find out what they're doing and stop it before they even knew we're alive."

From the expressions shown, my idea was met with general approval.

"Jess, can you do a soft recon of that town and give us more information without endangering yourself?" I asked.

My wife chewed a lip for a moment and then nodded. "Yes, I can do that. But it would help tremendously if I could see the place."

"Any maps of West Virginia?" I quorumed the group.

"In the RV," answered Mindy, getting comfortable on the floor. "Burned to ash."

Floating in closer, his feet tucked underneath his butt, Raul smiled. "There I can help. Mike? The hair."

Smiling in understanding, Donaher reached inside his cassock and withdrew a white evidence envelope. Using tweezers, he pulled into view the werewolf hairs he had found on the corpses on the highway. How long ago was that, a million years?

"Standard ritual?" asked Father Mike.

Horta nodded and we prepared for the long-distance call. This was not going to be an easy task for mage or telepath. There was a good thousand miles to cover, with nobody on the other end that either was familiar with, plus it was hostile country patrolled by an enemy telepath as strong as Jess. Maybe better. Just your average day on the job.

Clearing a spot in the wreckage, we laid a soft blanket on the floor and dimmed the lights. Placing the hairs in the middle of our circle, Raul began speaking under his breath, raising his voice in timbre and volume until he shouted the last unintelligible word and lightning crackled from his staff to hit the hair.

Whew! What a stink.

In ragged stages, a blob of light formed on the blanket, a splotch that moved and changed, flowed and re-formed until it suddenly clarified into an aerial view of Hadleyville and the surrounding country. It was primarily the same as we last saw it, with one notable exception.

The hotel was gone. Only a flat-bottomed hole remained to show where the ten-story structure had once been.

"Confirmation," I barked, staring at the translucent three-dimensional image. "Is this the past, present or future?"

"Present," cursed Raul, scrunching his face into a scowl.

Mindy picked at the vacant spot with the tip of her sword.

"Blown up?" she asked. "Teleported away? Eaten? What did they do with it, Ra?"

He gave a palms-up shrug. "There's no way of telling."

"Wait," said Jessica in a soft whispery voice. "There's a feeling there . . . a message . . ."

Eyebrows raised.

"A message from the Scion?" scoffed Mindy, amused.

Speaking quietly, so as not to disturb my wife's concentration, I explained. "Telepathic residue. Hadleyville is so twisted in the different dimensions, it would have been unusual to discover there wasn't any ghostly thought from the residents."

"It's very fuzzy . . . jumbled . . . chaotic . . ."

"That sounds like the Scion," agreed Raul.

Donaher rapped the mage on the head with his Bible. Horta got the hint. No jokes. This situation was too unclear. We needed information badly. Lots of it, and now. What was their master plan? Where was the Hadleyville Hotel? And what happened at the occult convention which started these events? Was it an isolated incident, or an event chain that we could somehow break?

"Mostly there's hate . . . ," whispered Jess, her vision turned to infinity. "And disgust at the decadence of the world . . ."

We exchanged glances. Could that be the big reason? The Scion were ethical purists and wanted to destroy the world because civilization was so decadent? And I'm Ethel Merman.

"But also a purpose . . . and much happiness . . . The Day is coming . . ."

That sounded bad. We could hear the capital letter.

"Which Day?" demanded Renault.

". . . soon . . . ," my wife breathed, and with a body jerk, Jessica returned to us.

"Good work, kid," I complimented, patting her knee.

She smiled, then went pale and clutched my arm. "Oh, Edwardo, they know who we are!"

"That we're Bureau 13?" asked Mindy, shocked.

"Say, that is bad news," agreed Raul.

My wife shook her head. "No! The Scion knows who *we* are."

"We, as in us?" asked Father Donaher, with no trace of his phony Irish accent.

"Our names?" squeaked Raul.

A frightened nod.

Mike and I crossed ourselves. Sitting side by side, Mindy and George bumped hands and I could have sworn they maintained the contact for a bit longer than decorum allowed.

"How?" asked Raul, his fingers clenching the staff lying across his knees.

"The license," explained Jessica wearily.

Eh? Ah! Oh. The license plates on our ex-van were Illinois and we had a Chicago sticker in the window. With that much info, tracking us was easy. I smacked fist into palm. Damnation! The team had been fighting nonsentient monsters for so long, we made a serious mistake. And in this business, one was all you got. On the other hand, what was the worst they could do with that information?

"Jessica, check our apartment!" cried Mindy.

Grabbing hold of the glowing necklace, my wife closed her eyes and frowned in concentration. "Somebody is there!"

"What?!" we bellowed in loose harmony.

"There are dead werewolves littering the floor," she spoke in a monotone. "They must have died by the dozens to gain entrance, but they did get in."

At least our defenses had held that much.

"Donaher!" I snapped. "Call both of our downstairs tenants and inform them the building is on fire. Order them out now! Save nothing! Just get out!"

"Done!" he cried, sprinting for the desk phone.

A towel wrapped around her head, and thankfully wearing a bathrobe, Tina had exited the bathroom during the shouting match. "What about deaf family on floor first," asked Blanco in concern. The deudonic pulses of her steel wand ebbed and sparked in mimicry of her emotional discord.

I waved the trifle aside. "They have a computer monitor hooked to the phone that allows them to see and read any incoming message. A flashing red light tells them the phone is ringing."

Father Donaher spun around. "George!"

"Yeah?"

"Ready the SDC!"

He gulped and got busy with the equipment bag. Soon, he handed me a miniature radio transmitter with a built-in keypad.

"Jess?" I asked, typing a long coded phrase into the minicomputer.

She released the gem. "Yes, the tenants are safe outside and the fire department is on the way. The monsters are rummaging through our computer file and—"

I hit the switch.

In a way, I was glad we couldn't see the results of that simple action. Our apartment building was designed by the Technical Services geniuses of the Bureau to be as fireproof as possible on the outside. The inside, however, was packed with enough thermite and napalm to make Hell feel embarrassed.

Tossing the SDC aside, I slumped in my chair. Jessica touched my arm and gave a squeeze. Mindy tightened her fists until the knuckles cracked. A solemn Donaher began saying his rosary. George closed his eyes. Raul was livid. Tina was pale.

Everything we owned was now gone. Our wedding album, family photos, Mindy's antique weapons collection, Raul's library on magic, our trophy room filled with irreplaceable mementoes from our combined ten years of service. Gone. Gone. What a day this had been! But at least it was over.

No, it isn't.

Good Lord, what now? An IRS audit?

We should be so lucky.

Uh-oh.

"We didn't get them all," announced Jessica aloud.

Groans greeted the statement.

"How many escaped?" asked Renault wearily, picking at some lint on his new slacks.

"No, we killed the werewolves in our apartment," corrected my wife. "But Hadleyville boasted a population of two thousand and we have only eliminated about a hundred."

"So it's not over yet," growled Mindy, partially drawing her sword and then slamming the blade back into the scabbard.

"Not by a long shot."

"What do you mean?"

"There's to be an attack on Bureau headquarters." My wife said it hesitantly, as if not sure she had that correct. "I was trying to scan their minds when the roof caved in, but I definitely got that much."

"Faith, lass, and how could they possibly find it?" countered Father Donaher. "We don't even know where HQ is!"

A reasonable question. Since the Slaughter of '77, when most of the Bureau got destroyed by an unknown enemy, not even its own agents knew where headquarters was located. I thought we had found it once in Manhattan, but by the next business day, it was gone.

"It doesn't matter," said Jess in that sad voice.

"What?"

"Eh?"

"Nonsense!"

"Why?" I demanded, getting to the heart of the matter.

"The exact location of the Bureau isn't pertinent to the attack," she wearily explained in a monotone. "Now that the Scion knows we come from Chicago, they plan to totally destroy the city. All of it. Every building, person, rock and tree. That way they're sure of getting our hidden main base."

Dead silence.

"But HQ may not even be in Chi!" stormed Renault. "It moves around, so this sort of thing can't happen!"

Raul scowled. "Try telling them that."

"When is the attack?" I asked breathlessly.

"Midnight."

"Tomorrow? Next week?" prompted Mindy, hoping.

Unfortunately, Jess gave the worst answer possible.

"Tonight," she said, gazing at the clock on the motel wall. "In four hours."

Tick-tick.

10

Within minutes after placing a telephone call to the local FBI office, a commandeered U.S. Army Huey helicopter retrieved us from the Lazy Eight Motel. Violating federal and civilian air traffic laws, the chopper ferried the team to the Lake City Arsenal, where a sleek USAF supersonic transport flew us back to Chicago. Traveling at Mach 4, we arrived almost as fast as Mr. Renault could drive.

En route we telephoned a travel agency and made reservations in our own names for a train to New York and chartered a plane to London, England. That was to throw the Scion off the trail. Underestimating these people was fast becoming a sure way to die.

Also, I sent a coded, scrambled radio message to our hidden headquarters detailing our discovery and the possible threat to Chicago. A special meeting was arranged at the downtown Sears Tower for nine o'clock, which would give us twenty minutes to examine the ruins of our apartment building for any clues or Scion survivors. Telepathic impressions were good, but if we could secure a prisoner and make the bum talk, we might bust this plan before fruition. That is, if winged hordes of flying Mack trucks didn't try to ram the plane in midflight. Luckily, there were no attacks and we arrived on schedule.

It made me nervous.

There was a big crowd of reporters at the main terminal, so we chatted with the O'Hare security and took a side route through the hangars and called a cab from there.

We saw the crowds from a block away. Police cars with flashing lights, fire trucks spewing streams of water at the crackling ruin of our decimated home. Parking at the corner, we paid off the car and proceeded on foot. Nobody said a word.

The marble outside of the building was black with soot. Every window was gone, the roof was missing and it was painfully obvious that the structure was now hollow.

Strong shoulders and grim determination got us through the bustling crowd of curious onlookers. A TV station was here filming the destruction, and maybe a dozen people in the crowd had cameras. Raul gestured with his "empty" hand and the TV camera geysered sparks. Tina subvocalized an unintelligible word and every camera in the crowd popped open, spilling rolls of film onto the ground. An ambulance was nearby and I saw our tenants getting treatment for smoke inhalation. Otherwise, everybody seemed fine. Our Bureau-issued insurance would cover medical expenses, replace their stuff and pay ample punitive for relocating. Even if we survived this night and rebuilt the place, I made a solemn vow never to have tenants again. It was too damn dangerous.

FBI badges allowed us passage past the police cordon, and a telepathic suggestion from Jessica convinced the fire captain to let us by the sweaty, tired firemen.

Picking our way through the jumble of fire hoses, safety barriers, pools of water and foam, we stepped into the thermal ruins. Destruction was rampant. Great slabs of concrete were piled atop each other, bits of furniture smoldered with flame. Glancing up, I could faintly see the stars through the thick smoke rising from a thousand small blazes still crackling. The heat was intense, the cloying smoke thick enough to chew. Horta regulated the temperature and Tina cleaned the air. Father Donaher did a blessing and George kept guard with his banjo. I cursed. Our home was gutted to the walls.

"Our home," sniffed Blanco.

A smoking timber fell from the sky directly towards us.

"Yeck. What a mess," said Mindy, batting the hundred-pound piece of charcoal away with her sword. The neatly twained pieces hit a pile of wet foam to expose the red embers underneath.

Ed, sent Jess.

"Yes?" I asked aloud, using my shoe to push about an unbroken dinner plate on the soiled terrazzo. Wow. Must be that Corel style.

Pirate Pete is gone.

"Really can't blame him," remarked George, nudging a charred section of flooring with the muzzle of his M-60. "What self-respecting ghost would want to stay in a dump like this?"

"No," said Father Donaher, his body stiff with rage. "There has been an exorcism."

I started to ask why, but the reason was obvious. We wanted prisoners to talk and they wanted the same. But I would get good money that the old buccaneer who lived in our cellar had probably put up a magnificent fight before the Scion finally drove him into the Great Abyss from which nobody ever returns.

Obviously, the Scion telepath had gotten more from us in Hadleyville than we had imagined. Okay, he/she/it would be the first to die.

"Another score to settle with these brigands," growled Mindy.

Tina agreed, bolts of lightning playing about her partially recharged staff. I gave her a nudge to make her stop that. Too many witnesses.

With a gasp of delight, Raul pulled an undamaged volume from a pile of embers. The book promptly disintegrated into ash.

"Enough searching for physical clues," I commanded, dusting off my hand. "Let's do a full globular sweep. Psionics, ethereal, mystic and EM scan."

Devices were activated, spells unleashed, wands waved. To the grand sum total result of nothing. The Scion covered their tracks well.

Pocketing my scanner, I sighed in resignation. "Let's go."

As we departed the burnt shell of a building, George retrieved a broken closet door from a pile of bed frames and jimmied it into a sagging doorway. Team Tunafish left home for the very last time.

Weary and angry, we moved resolutely through the crowd of puzzled people trying to shove uncooperative film back into cameras. Heading uptown, the team hung a right. No sense trying to get a cab for seven people when the Sears Tower was only a few blocks away.

Once past the hubbub, the streets of Chi were almost entirely deserted at this hour. Elsewhere, the joints may be jumping, but we midwesterners like to get our sleep. In the far distance, a lonely Pace bus was rumbling along its night-owl route. Wisps of steam rose from the manhole covers dotting the street and you could hear the streetlights click as they went from red to green.

"Holy jamoke!" cried a voice. "It's them!"

We spun about. Across the street was a delivery truck with its rear flap rolled up and a score of men and women with their backs to us, lifting boxes into the vehicle. Their auras were human so I relaxed. Oh hell. What now? A news team?

"Jamoke?" queried Mindy with a smile.

Donaher scowled. "Faith, that's a mining term, isn't it?"

"I can't sense them," said Jess with urgency in her voice.

. . . and the group pivoted towards us with machine guns blazing. Shit!

Tracers filled the air. Donaher was slammed against the wall, blood sprayed from Blanco's left arm and something punched me in the stomach. Reaching upward, Mindy grabbed my belt and yanked me to the pavement behind a parked car. The sidewalk felt rough and cool against my cheek.

Tracer rounds filled the air. Windows exploded. Ricochets blew stone chips off the brick wall behind us. Parked cars bucked from the multiple impact of heavy-caliber bullets. Rolling onto my knees, I drew both Magnums and smelled gasoline.

"Hut! Hut! Hut!" I cried in a new battle phrase inspired by some old foes. Dead and buried, thankfully.

Rolling to new positions, the first car whoofed into

flames. We waited the standard six seconds, then popped up and returned the gunplay in an orchestrated attack pattern. Six of the people shooting at us hit the ground in a manner to suggest that they were definitely going to stay there. But the rest stood brazen, uncaring of the lead and silver fusillade slamming into them.

Then they started to grow in size. Seams split as limbs expanded. Coats of hair sprouted, and toothy snouts extended. Ears went pointed. Hands became paws.

In seconds, the remnants of their shirts and dresses were fluttering to the ground. But instead of being naked, each creature was wearing a SWAT-style full-body flak jacket.

Aiming with extreme care, I pumped six rounds into the chest of one of them. The man-beast didn't even stagger from the trip-hammer blows of the .357 slugs. Our rounds couldn't penetrate their body armor.

Hoo boy.

With a bow twang, Mindy put an arrow into one of their eyes. Startled, the man paused and yanked the shaft free, snapping the hard wood between hoary talons. Raul sent a Lightning Bolt their way and a werewolf crackled into ash. Another took her place. George added a concentrated burst from the M-60, making their delivery van detonate.

Light and thunder filled the street, and as the force of the blast slowly dissipated vision returned.

Dripping flame, they started towards us.

What the hell?

They're coated with Cosmoline, sent Jess. *A thermal-resistant chemical compound that stage magicians use so they can hold burning coals in the palm of their hand.*

"Limitations?" asked Donaher, ramming fresh shells into his shotgun. The rosary wrapped around his hand clinked with every round. Bureau body armor showed through the hole in his cassock.

It'll wear off in about an hour. And there's a good chance of cancer within five years.

"We're in trouble!" I announced to the rest of the team in case they had not been paying close attention. I swallowed and commanded myself not to barf. Geez, my stomach hurt!

Store windows were gone. Alarms were clanging. Lights were coming on in a hundred windows. A crowd was starting to gather. The police would be here in about thirty seconds.

"If we had some explosives, we could blow the flak jackets off and then shoot 'em," stated George, peppering a werewolf with .30 silver bullets. The soft metal rounds simply flattened against the military flak jackets and stayed there. The linked belt of ammo dangling from his machine rifle was shrinking fast.

Livid, Jessica was staring at the monsters. Whether she was trying to Brain Blast them, steal information, redirect the police or shoo away civilians, I didn't know. But I hoped all four. And maybe a fifth.

"Any grenades?" asked Tina, casting a Death spell. The chosen target went stiff and keeled over with a lily in its paws. Nice touch.

Pockets were patted. "No."

"Used mine already," said Father Donaher through clenched teeth.

"Yes!" cried Jennings. Ripping at her wrist, she removed her Bureau watch, buckled the strap tight around the shaft of an arrow. Setting the self-destruct, she stood, released the shaft and ducked again.

Dead center, the arrow went deep into the chest of a charging werewolf. Terrified, the man-beast stopped and was trying to pull the shaft free when it exploded. When the smoke cleared, I saw his chest was bare fur. Yowsa! I gave him three silver hollow-points smack in the aorta. Coughing blood, he stumbled backwards, turned into a human and died.

Six more watches were thrust at Jennings.

The rest of the pack started running.

Magnums at the ready, I stood. Wild shadows danced everywhere from the burning vehicles, making it hard to see. But Mindy got two additional werewolves before they disappeared down a dark alleyway.

"George on cover! Donaher bandage Tina. Raul, teleport them out of here! Jess and Mindy with me!"

The team split. Dashing across the littered street, I jumped over a smoking tire and dodged round a naked corpse. We were going to get one of these bastards alive. Or die trying.

"On point," I called as we reached the other sidewalk. Mindy and Jess separated, each going to a side of the alley. I stood in the middle of the entrance, then slowly walked in. Jess and Mindy slipped round the corners and hugged the walls.

As befitting a center city alley, it was wide, filled with garbage and should have been well lit. Had the Scion removed the bulbs to establish a retreat? They were good. But were they really that good?

With each passing minute, the werewolves could be getting further and further away. I would have loved to simply chase right after them like the idiots in the movies. But that was how good cops got their names in granite.

"Blood," whispered a shadow the size and shape of Jennings.

As she gave no additional information, that meant we were headed in the correct direction.

"Jessica?" I asked in my head.

They're psi-shielded, she responded. *I can't even detect their physical presence. But I'm trying to probe around and locate a dead spot where I can't sense anything.*

I understood that. A mental shield that's 100 percent effective is not there. So you look for what's not there.

We passed a favorite Chinese restaurant, the rich smells completely masking the pungent aromas of the alley. Not a single beam of light reached the dark alleyway from that boisterous establishment.

Hey, since when do restaurants paint their rear windows over?

"Alert," I said.

Danger, sent Jess.

"Incoming," said Mindy.

In an oft-practiced move, we took refuge behind garbage cans and Dumpsters. A tiny pinprick of light appeared in the distant blackness, which rapidly swelled in size until a glaring ring of exhaust painfully washed over us as a HAFLA missile streaked by.

One . . . two . . . three . . . and a strident explosion illuminated the alley behind us, burning garbage spewed into the sky like trashy fireworks. However, the brief flash showed a dozen more werewolves ahead of us entrenched atop a law office.

Okay, so it was a trap. Great. Those can work both ways.

I tracked to the logical vector of launching and pumped a few rounds that way, with Jessica's Uzi also saying hello. A chattering barrage of machine-gun bullets answered our question.

The door to the Chinese restaurant opened a crack, bathing us in brilliant light. Jessica barked something in Mandarin. The door slammed shut, was bolted, and I heard scraping noises as if a piece of furniture was being shoved against the portal.

"What the hell did you say?" I asked, reloading fast.

Tong war.

Ah. Good choice.

There was a twang alongside me, and something on the dark roof ahead exploded into flame and fur. I emptied both pistols at that locale and got a death howl as a reward.

Another rocket came streaking in to impact slightly in front of us. The blast knocked me off my feet and I couldn't feel my left arm. That meant a bad wound.

Ed, I don't think prisoners is an option anymore.

"Why?" I demanded, struggling to my knees and holding a Magnum in my armpit so I could slip in the last speedload of silver bullets. "Not that I disagree, but why do you say so?"

There was a helicopter parked on the roof. I have already killed the pilot, but the copilot is still active.

Pause.

She slammed a fresh clip into the Uzi and pulled the bolt. *Plus it has a 40mm Vulcan mini-cannon.*

Oh fudge.

There was a scattering of reddish light from the missile hits ahead and behind our Dumpster. In that dark alleyway we were bracketed with deadly illumination. Already it was possible to faintly discern us. The next rocket would be the last.

"Saigon bug-out," I ordered, getting ready to make a run for safety. Oh well, can't win 'em all.

"No frigging way," said Jennings loud and clear, and she stepped into the middle of the alleyway, the distant fires bathing her in flickering illumination. Bullets started to chew the alley around her, but Jennings just stood there, bow in hand.

With a revving whine, I heard the helicopter gunship start to spin its rotor blades preparing for takeoff and a strafing run. Oh hell. Then my Bureau sunglasses came alive, the whole edge of the roof of the law office plainly highlighted in the infrared spectrum by the massive thermal outpouring from the big helicopter engines.

Mindy notched an arrow in her bow and waited.

The black outlines of two werewolves started angling their machine guns in an overlapping figure-eight pattern, while another outline stood with a squat tube in its paws. He flipped the sights, zeroed the port and aimed the gaping end of the tube in our direction.

Jennings released her shaft.

There was a double explosion as the wristwatch on the arrow detonated the LAW still in its launching tube. The results of the combination were spectacular. A thundering fireball engulfed the howling werewolves, blowing furry bodies off the building, and as the chopper tried for a lift-off it also blew apart, adding the destructive power of its fuel and ammunition to the brewing hellstorm on the roof.

So much for prisoners.

Watching the mushroom cloud of smoke rise into the starry sky, I felt the normally high level of my confidence slip a notch. Werewolves with flak jackets and military weapons. This was beyond serious. Maybe these bozos actually were going to try to destroy Chicago. And maybe even succeed.

"Ed, we need help," said Mindy, hobbling close.

Accepting a wristwatch, I heartily agreed.

"And who ya gonna call?" asked Jess with a weak grin.

Jennings started to speak, then stopped. Nyah. Besides, they only worked the East Coast.

Activating my watch, I began the procedure to relay a priority-one call to Bureau HQ. Who was I going to summon for assistance?

Everybody.

11

"Who the hell are you?" demanded the grizzled police captain as I entered the conference room of City Hall.

"In charge," I snapped, settling the matter at once. Oozing confidence, I strode up the center aisle between a sea of folding chairs filled with law enforcement personnel from a dozen federal, state and city organizations. And in my hand was written permission from Horace Gordon to tell these people anything necessary.

Including the awful truth.

When we arrived at the Sears Tower, Horace Gordon himself was waiting for us. Doc Robertson and his field forensic team analyzed the remains of the people who attacked us on State Street, and the results were most interesting. The humans who died so easily from our bullets were local gangsters who dealt in stolen munitions and military weapons. No shit. And the pilot in the illegally armed helicopter was Jim "Mad Dog" Kerigan, a professional mercenary. News that cheered nobody. The Scion was hitting us with everything they could. I debated on requesting the Chicago PD to keep an extra-special watch on the import or sales of any kitchen sinks.

The most disturbing news was that the alarms on the synchronized digital wristwatches of everybody, human and in-, had been set for exactly five minutes till midnight. Giving them just enough time to do what, leave town? Ominous.

Most of my team stayed to brief the other Bureau 13 teams called in on this emergency, and I was given the honor of lying to six thousand trained observers.

Whee, what fun.

Taking the podium on the raised speaker's platform, I opened my attaché case and glanced at the wall clock: 9:10.

Before me was a resolute battalion of grim faces. There was a neatly pressed platoon of suits with flesh-colored wires snaking out of their ears and down into the stiff shirt collars: U.S. Secret Service. Smart and tough, although slightly fanatical about America, they were the best pistol marksmen in the world.

Nearby was a gang of FBI agents wearing our official blue suit and matching tie. We nodded at each other. I had dealt with Stan and his people before. Their only knowledge of me was as the-guy-who-showed-up-when-the-shit-hit-the-fan. How true.

Filling the front of each quarter area of chairs were the representatives of the military, the stiffly formal operatives in full-dress uniforms: Army Intelligence, Air Force Intelligence and Naval Intelligence.

Sitting alone were the field commanders of the Green Berets, Navy SEALS and Air Force Rangers. The two men and a woman seemed entirely at ease, but that was normal. These folk were trained never to get nervous or frightened. In a crashing plane full of dynamite, they would finish their card game and then jump naked into enemy territory.

Ice. They were made of solid ice.

By the window, a lone woman in a plain dress was wearing a governmental pass identifying her as CIA. Legally, the Company was not allowed to operate within the continental boundaries of the United States, but that had never stopped them before.

The rest of the attendees were mostly composed of the top echelon from the State Police, Chicago city police, sheriff's office and Federal Sky Marshals. I do believe there was a smattering of National Guard officers and Coast Guard captains as well.

Lounging in a corner was as disreputable a collection of scum and assorted miscreants as it has ever been my misfortune to encounter. Bums, bag ladies, whores and pimps, they even had a small runny-nosed child with them to complete that nice Amish family ensemble. I could almost smell the filth on their bodies and started to scratch at the fleas I mentally felt.

Of course, the impression was totally wrong. Half of them were undercover DEA agents and the rest were volunteer members of the MTA's elite transit police, code-named CATs—Criminal Attack Team. These folk loitered about in sewers and alleyways, and the instant they saw a crime starting to be committed, they jumped the perp. CATs were more interested in stopping the occurrence of a crime than bagging collars and looking good to the chief so they could get promoted out of the CAT squad. Hell, you had to wait on a list and pass tests to get into it! And the child was actually a midget who held black belts in enough different styles of the martial arts to give Mindy a good fight.

That's when I noticed . . . him.

Standing by the door was a solitary figure in a rumpled blue outfit. He was unshaven, smoking a cigar, and radiated power and authority. I was damned if I could identify what branch of the Justice Department he came from. TLF? Treasury Department? Another covert agency like our own? I went for the gold.

"Who are you?" I demanded.

The big man removed the cigar from his mouth and gazed at the glowing tip before answering, obviously marshaling his collection of responses for the correct reply.

"Janitor," he said at last. "Youse goit nuff cha'rs?"

I nodded yes and shooed him away. Mentally, I made a personal note to burn my private investigator's license when I got home. Oops, too late.

Finished shuffling my papers into the correct order, I turned around. On the wall behind me was a huge pull-down map of Chicago and its suburbs. Yanking on the bottom bar, I eased the map upward to expose the words "four million," which Mindy had carved into the cinder blocks with her amazing sword. Involuntarily, I glanced at my hands. Boy, was that thing sharp.

"That," I boomed at them over the loudspeaker system, "is precisely why we are here. The four million residents of greater Chicagoland." Which is what we locals called the whole damn shebang of our mighty metropolis. Had to let the gang know I was not some thirty-day wonder from DC here to steal the glory. I was a Looper, with family and friends only blocks away.

A small hand was raised for a question. I hate such formality, but in this situation it seemed the only way to control the possible pandemonium. I gestured at the child.

"How come you're dressed like FBI?" asked the CAT, squinting suspiciously at me.

"Now, that's a damn fool question, don't you think?" I growled at him in my best impersonation of Horace Gordon.

Chuckles sounded from everybody but the military.

"Yeah, I guess," he relented.

I cleared my throat. "Firstly, as of twenty-one hundred this day, the President of the United States, in conjunction with Congress, has placed the city of Chicago under martial law."

Shocked murmurs even came from the military with that announcement. Except for the Special Forces gang. Ice.

"However," I continued, "this ploy is only a political move to legally save our butts if we screw up big-time. Should this deal come off as planned, nobody is the wiser and the media never finds out."

Pensive faces. Hushed conversations. Grudging acceptance.

From the attaché case, I slid a piece of paper into a slot on the podium. "The enemy calls itself the SSD," I began.

The Scion of the Silver Dagger, I thought, was a bit too far out for even this veteran group to handle in a single dose.

"Okay, we call 'em Sid," stated a DEA.

I nodded. Give the enemy a silly name and you remove half of their power to frighten. God, I love professionals.

"Sid has sworn to destroy Chicago."

The State Police raised her hand.

"Yes, they're serious," I cut her off. "And competent enough to do it. They have already annihilated a small town in West Virginia just to test their equipment."

What's a lie among friends?

"Any survivors?" asked the Secret Service.

I gave them a full eight-second dramatic pause. "No."

A room of furrowed brows and grimly set jaws. I could see the thought process in their faces. First blood went to the enemy. The Scion was just elevated to a real threat. But that wasn't enough. Time to drive the stake home.

"In point of fact," I continued, "Sid is so competent that the military has already invaded Chi with hundreds of plain-clothes soldiers, plus the President of the United States has ordered the Pentagon to activate the North America defense grid, placing NORAD and SAC on DefCon Two."

That sobered a lot of them.

A Sky Marshal whistled. "One step from war."

"Now you're starting to get the picture," I informed them.

"Sid is as dangerous as they come. Smart, ruthless and very well trained. With more equipment than we like to think about."

"Where did they get it?" asked the Coast Guard.

"Handled already," I snapped. Didn't want them trying to ferret out the Scion by backtracking their equipment. They might discover the Bureau!

"How do they plan to destroy Chicago?" asked Air Force Intel. "A nuclear device?"

Device. Didn't anybody say "bomb" anymore?

"Unknown," I replied honestly. "But if they got one, they will use it. Even if a hundred of their own people are within the main fireball."

"Loonies," noted a city cop clinically.

"Fanatics," I corrected. "Doped on combat drugs, which gives them twice normal human strength."

How else was I to explain paranormal strength? Say they

visited the health spa regularly? Watched Arnold Schwarzenegger movies?

The military was remarkably complacent during this, but I did notice a few generals dictating notes into pocket recorders. Futile. Any recording leaving this room would be instantly erased. And if they had some secret lab invent the drug, we'd only steal it again like we did the last four.

"Plus Sid has special body armor that regulation police rounds will not penetrate," I went on.

A few rueful smiles.

"Nor will illegal dumdum rounds or those Teflon-coated European bullets do shit to these guys."

The smiles melted.

I jerked a thumb towards the boxes of ammunition stacked along the wall. "However, over there are a few thousand rounds of Top Secret plasma bullets. They're steel-jacketed hollow points with a liquid-silver metal core. The rounds will easily go through the flak jackets and then explode."

"No shit?" asked the CIA, raising an eyebrow.

"No shit," I informed her steadfastly.

The DEA wino chuckled. "Cops with silver bullets. Hi-ho, Tonto! Away . . ."

Whew. At least they were thinking Lone Ranger and not werewolves.

"How very amusing," I said in a voice guaranteed to tell them it was anything but.

"What's the timetable?" asked the FBI. "How long do we have to prepare before they attack?"

Although wearing a watch, I purposely glanced at the clock on the wall. "Roughly two hours twenty minutes. They strike at midnight."

Eyes went wide, but only silence greeted my outrageous statement. My respect grew. In their faces, I could see the crowd weigh options and discard useless procedures. Evacuating the city was a laugh. The Bureau had tried that once when New York was in serious danger and more people died in the exodus than from the enemy.

"And this is the earliest you could inform us?" admonished the National Guard furiously.

Four-second pause. "Yes."

"This midnight deadline," asked one of the CATs, "is it a lock?"

"Dead certain."

Army Intelligence smiled. "Sir, why don't we let them know that we know and maybe that'll scare 'em off, or at least slow the bastards down a bit."

"Nice try," I acknowledged. "But Sid does know that we know and doesn't give a good goddamn."

"They really think they can pull it off," said Naval Intelligence slowly. Her uniform proclaimed she was in the submarine corps. "Destroy Chicago?"

"To the ground," I reiterated as firmly as possible.

A Green Beret colonel scratched his dimpled chin. "Or from the ground up," he murmured thoughtfully.

That was an interesting idea.

"Two hours doesn't give us much time," observed the CAT midget, lighting a pipe. "It's going to be a bitch following standard police procedure."

I was prepared for this.

"Fuck procedure," I told them bluntly. "Blow your covers, strong-arm suspects, enter houses without warrants, do whatever you have to."

The clock on the wall loudly clicked forward another minute.

"Because we're rapidly running out of time. And there are four million innocent people who have placed their trust and their lives in our hands."

"And when we find Sid?" asked the bag lady, checking the clip in her Gloch 10mm automatic pistol. A calloused thumb started ejecting rounds as a prelude to reloading.

This was no time to mince words. Not only might it get in the way, but being diplomatic could very seriously lower the high intensity of feeling I desperately needed to instill into this group. Especially that particular team of police officers.

When the CATs prowled the city, street crime dropped like a rock.

"If you find them," I said coldly, "blow their frigging brains out. We neither want nor need prisoners."

Besides, I wasn't sure we could handle any.

A representative of Air Force Rangers stood up. "I am not thrilled by the concept of armed personnel running amuck in a major city with a government license to kill randomly."

I spoke from the heart. "If you blow away some poor slob by accident, it will be a terrible shame. But accidents happen. However, if anybody—repeat, anybody—uses this emergency as an opportunity to take a little personal vengeance, he or she will answer to me and my people, who do not legally exist and have no board of inquiry to explain their actions to."

Bodies relaxed. They now understood that this was not to be a free-for-all, but a deadly serious gambit to save a city from extinction. Step one: save Chicago. Step two would be to justify our actions to a population still sucking in air.

"Alert," said a Secret Service, touching his ear. "There has just been an attempt to seize control of the U.S.S. *Idaho* while on a training cruise in Lake Michigan."

"The *Idaho*?" snapped an admiral. "That's an antique!"

The CIA frowned. "But secretly armed with Tomahawk nuclear missiles."

Shocked murmurs engulfed the room.

"You know about that, huh?" asked the admiral.

A grim nod.

"As of five minutes ago, a squadron of Army Apache helicopters in a joint operation with Air Force B-52 fighter/bombers had sunk the *Idaho* with concentrated missile fire," continued the Secret Service agent. "Rescue operations by the Coast Guard are proceeding for the crew."

The Navy SEAL touched his ear. "The warheads are safe. My people have them."

A SWAT crossed himself. The CIA took the bottle of whiskey from the DEA wino and downed a healthy shot. I agreed with the sentiment. Dear God, oh dear loving God. The fight for Chicago had already begun.

Hours ahead of schedule.

12

Two seconds later, the meeting was over, with everybody politely filing out of the room so that they could start unleashing their hordes of destruction. When it was just me alone, I touched the shiny new bracelet on my wrist and Jumped to the top floor of the Sears Tower.

I appeared inside a pentagram made of yellow marking tape on the carpeted floor. On every side I was banked by sandbag walls abristle with machine guns, arbalists, microwave beamers and other assorted deathdealers.

A pistol lowered. "It's Ed!"

The safety was clicked off an Uzi. "It only looks like Ed."

"Horatio," I said fast.

"Cerberus."

"Balder."

"Right," I said, finishing the litany of famous guards.

A section of the sandbags moved backwards on hidden rollers and I scooted free. I shook hands with some folk I knew and was given a Kirlian security badge. It glowed visibly with my normally hidden aura. Also had my name and thumbprint.

Following the markers on the floor, I moved through the bustling crowd of humans and supernaturals, nearly getting trampled by Clarmont the gorgon and his lovely wife, Boom.

Passing another checkpoint, I was scanned by a team of folk holding a machine which resembled a leaf blower and was finally admitted into the main conference hall of the Tower.

Going through the double sets of sliding doors, I stepped into Madhouse Central. Dimly illuminated, the four walls of the big room displayed vector graphics of the different sections of Chicago. Moving colored dots, triangles and other geometric figures indicated police, possible monster attacks and Bureau teams.

Clustered on the floor were banks of control boards filled with radar screens, thermographs from orbital satellites, rainbow swirls of chemical readouts and the dancing light show of Kirlian television. A very recent invention, it had already stopped two transdimensional invasions and gotten four talk show hosts fired and/or jailed.

Lounging against the back wall was a delicious assortment of women. Two were wearing full evening gowns, one was a cop, another a cabdriver, and the last was in a spandex jumpsuit which couldn't show more of her anatomy if she had been naked. These were the ThunderBunnies, the sole Bureau 13 team for the entire state of Texas.

The whole staff of a Houston brothel had been violently introduced to the world of the supernatural when a client had turned out to be an incubus, or sex vampire, and these ladies of the evening had to become impromptu defenders of a sleeping town and save the population from being . . . ah, enjoyed to death, by him and his female counterpart, a succubus.

Now, that was a story worth telling and retelling around the fireplace at two in the morning. Just send the kids to bed first.

Near them was a somber crowd of men and women. Team Maccabees. Some had beards and long sideburns with the fringe at the belt. Others merely wore yarmulkes, the brimless skullcaps. But tonight each was sporting combat armor and automatic weapons. Even the cabalistic mage, although he did it to fool the opposition and only carried the weapon as a spare for the fighters. Good thinking, actually. The Bureau jokingly referred to them as the American Mossad. Their information-gathering system on the supernatural was so efficient, sometimes they informed HQ about a coming problem, instead of vice versa. And although they didn't like it, Maccabees would work on the Sabbath. What could be more holy than saving lives?

Their sad expresions tonight were directly attributable to

their missing telepathic leader, who died with the rest of the mentalists when this whole mess began.

Bandaging wounds and drinking Healing potions was our infamous gang of bad boys, Roger's Rangers. The Boston team broke rules that hadn't even been written yet, but they always got their monsters. Unfortunately, civilians had this nasty habit of getting dead by standing in the wrong place at the wrong time, and nothing the Rangers did had any effect on it. Some agents believed them to be cursed.

"Hey, Rangers!" I called out in passing.

The group pivoted with weapons, then relaxed when they saw it was only me.

"The *Idaho*?" I asked.

Wet and bloody, they nodded.

"Good job."

The eight Rangers shrugged.

Next came the Los Angeles branch: Team Angel. Their leader was a wild-haired man named Damon who posed as a science fiction author. His lieutenant was a dashingly handsome computer journalist only known as Aki. Finnish, I think. I waved hi to a beautiful woman in a low-cut gypsy gown of a thousand colors. Pat smiled in return and touched her nose. We both grinned at the private joke.

However, levity faded when I noticed standing over in a corner by himself a slender pale-skinned man, dressed in a black suit, white shirt with a white tie. He was smoking a pungent cigarette and had his hat pulled so low over his face that only a pair of eerie transparent blue eyes were visible beneath the rim.

It was the legendary J. P. Withers himself. The very first Bureau 13 agent recruited back in 1850. It was rumored that he was immortal and slightly insane. He had this very bad habit of using explosives when diplomacy would have done the job. Or using ten sticks of dynamite when one would have sufficed. Overkill wasn't his modus operandi, it was his philosophy of life. Rare indeed was the situation which warranted the summoning of J. P., and I was of the personal opinion that Horace Gordon was secretly terrified of the man. If man he was.

However, Withers was on our side. Mostly.

And in the center of the room, talking on two phones at the same time, was the chief: Horace Gordon.

A giant of a man, Gordon had gray crew-cut hair and a barely healed scar across his throat. The scar was new. He was dressed in black military boots and a tan NASA jumpsuit. A double holster was about his waist, with a laser pistol in the left and a short golden wizard wand in the right. How he could safely mix magic and technology was beyond me. Around his neck was an amulet on a silver chain that pulsed with protective blue anti-magic.

Then I found my own team, gleefully in the process of looting the collection of folding tables bowing under the weight of the massive assortment of weapons and magical supplies piled on top.

"Hey," I offered as greeting.

With cries of delight, they scampered close. Nothing like a good hug to help lower the tension.

Jessica was in denim pants, white shirt and denim short jacket. She had a double-barrel taser stun gun at her belt, an Uzi slung over her shoulder, and was arranging medical supplies inside a field surgery kit. The necklace was where it should be, dangling betwen her breasts and glowing contentedly. I would too.

Mindy was in her ninja outfit of loose black pajamas—no belt—with a double quiver of arrows on her back and a compound bow slung over her shoulders. Sword in hand, Jennings was stuffing knives into a sleeve.

Adjusting the rosary dangling from his belt, Father Mike was also in military fatigues. His combat Bible was in a holster at his hip, and over his back was a set of pressurized tanks, whose complex pipes fed into the short insulated sprayer discolored from heat. The M1A flamethrower was the big priest's favorite weapon when battling hellspawn or thawing frozen Thanksgiving turkeys. These tanks were an odd color, though.

"What's this?" I asked, thumbing the pressure rig with a fist.

"Amen," mumbled Donaher, kissing the rosary. "Hey, Ed.

Normally, I use jellied gasoline. But for this wee scenario, the tanks are filled with Napalm 4."

Patiently, I waited for enlightenment.

"Napalm 1 was jellied gasoline," he explained. "Number 2 could burn under water. Number 3 stuck to the target like epoxy glue."

"Number 4 does everything, I suppose."

"Aye, lad. And it's poisoned."

I made a face. "Very nasty, Michael."

He shrugged, making the tanks slosh. "If this helps to send more Scion members to meet their Maker, then praise the Lord."

When a Catholic priest starts talking like a Southern Baptist minister, I know we're in for trouble. Or a picnic.

"Hallelujah!" shouted Mindy.

Raul chuckled appreciatively. For some bizarre reason, Mr. Horta was in white, from deck shoes to nautical cap. Staff in hand, lumpy pouches hung over each shoulder, and his arms were full of copper bracelets. His pants pocket bulged with a hip flask and his linen shirt was embroidered with the words "shiver me timbers . . . what does that mean anyway?"

When had this sailing craze overcome him?

You gave him the Old Spice for his birthday, dear.

True enough. My fault, then.

Her long blond hair tied in a ponytail, Tina was in a tight Danceskin that changed color to match anything she stood near. A belt of small pouches went around her trim waist and a bandolier of foot-long magical wands draped across her chest. A few I could identify as Lightning or Flesh-to-Stone, the rest were unknowns. Even the butterfly on her cheek was wearing armor.

Whistling contentedly, George was adjusting the straps of his huge plastic backpack. The squarish container had a cushioned hip rest and padded shoulder hooks to help distribute the tremendous weight of the eighteen thousand rounds of ammo in the pack. From the top of the container snaked an enclosed belt which fed directly into the breech mechanism of a stocky rifle with a worn, pitted maw.

The Masterson assault cannon fired 20mm caseless, armor-piercing, high-explosive rounds. I have seen just one of these weapons destroy a whole company of giant robot spiders. Thankfully in another dimension. If news of this terrible gun was ever made public, Geneva would hold another convention just to outlaw the thing. Bureau regulations strictly forbade its use outside of a war.

Amigo was belly-up on the table, sawing toothpicks.

"Where's mine?" I asked eagerly. "Did it arrive?"

George took me by the elbow. "Over here. When the Rangers saw the rifle, they tried to confiscate it. But Raul and I convinced them that wasn't a great idea."

"That's right, pardner," growled Raul in the very worst John Wayne impersonation I ever heard. "Wa-ha."

Aside from my twin Magnums and a sampling of high explosives, in unrestricted combat I also carry a combo pack: three LAW rocket launchers and two HAFLA incendiary rockets in a cushioned haversack. But downtown Chicago was no place for a bazooka battle, as I knew from hard experience, so I had requisitioned the next best thing.

A Barrett rifle. There was no model number.

Longer than the M-60 and heavier than sin, the tremendous rifle was made exclusively of space-age alloys to cut the weight as much as possible. Chambered for .50 Long SuperMagnums, the rifle had a muzzle blast of 5,487 fps and an effective range of two incredible miles.

Cresting the main barrel was a Starlite sniper scope so sensitive that you could see the enemy's tonsils, in pitch-darkness, at nine hundred yards. The dictionary-size ammo clip held eleven of the gigantic cigar bullets. Twelve, if you were foolish, or desperate enough to carry this portable howitzer with a live round in the chamber.

I slid in the twelfth round.

"Tunafish!" called out Gordon, waving a hand, and we hurried over.

"How'd the briefing go?" asked the chief as a greeting. Signing a spell book, he handed it to thin air, where the volume vanished.

Quickly, I slid on my sunglasses, then yanked them off as

tears rolled down my cheeks. Zounds! Maximum overload.
Too much magic around here. Alvarez, never do that again.

"Well?" Horace repeated.

"Everybody is as ready as they can be on such short notice," I reported, wiping my eyes. "They each were handed a
copy of the written notice, and know they should report on
radio channel such and such, and that you'll issue orders that
damn well better be obeyed on channel such and such."

"Such and such?" queried Blanco.

Renault rested an arm around her curves. "It's a technical
term, sweetheart. Sort of like blah-blah, or thingy."

Lord, give me strength. "How about us, sir?" I asked.
"What's the status on our Wave division? And the Cyber-
Cops?"

"The mermaids have already been briefed and are taking
position out in Lake Michigan," said Gordon. "Our sentient
machines are in position at Hadleyville still searching for
clues to where that hotel went."

"Then we agree that it is the key to this whole matter?"
asked Raul.

The chief gave him a stare to wilt flowers on wallpaper.
"Was there ever any doubt?"

"Sir! Anti-yes. Sir!"

Having dealt with mages before, Gordon was nonplussed.
"Anyway, General MacAdams and the Phoenix team
have been split in half. One section positioned near Chey-
enne Mountain in case the Scion tried to infiltrate the base
and start a nuclear war."

"And the other half?"

"Is currently at Camp David with the President in case the
Scion has any ideas of taking the boss hostage and offering
his life in exchange for Bureau 13."

My temples started to throb. Ye god, what a devious mind
the chief had. But then, that's why he was in charge.

"Who does that leave to guard headquarters?" asked
Mindy bluntly.

Gordon looked at her askance. "Us," he replied.

That took a minute to sink in.

"It's here?" I gasped. "You moved Bureau HQ from . . .

wherever to here?" I had trouble getting the word out of my mouth.

"Saints preserve us, man, are you mad?" demanded Donaher in a booming voice.

Talking stopped in the room and J. P. Withers started our way.

"The purpose of the Bureau is to guard American citizens," started Horace coldly. "And our HQ has many devices and weapons which cannot safely or quickly be removed from . . . the place that we used to occupy."

"So you moved the whole base to exactly where the enemy thinks it is, so that we can better guard Chicago."

He seemed surprised at our reactions. "Of course. Contingency plans have been prepared in case we all die. But the best hope we have of not dying is to hit the Scion with everything we have."

"And that includes me," whispered Withers.

He stood near, but not close to us. Hands in pockets and the same cigarette smoking away at the same length.

Jessica gave a delicate cough. "Do you mind extinguishing that, please?" she asked politely.

Withers stared at my wife and, for a second, I thought he was going to kill her.

"If it accomodates you, madam," he relented, and drawing the smoking cigarette into his mouth, he chewed for a moment and swallowed.

Hoo boy.

A centaur in a flak jacket galloped by and tossed a folder towards the chief. "Sir, report on the *Idaho*!" And he galloped away.

Horace made the catch and flipped to page one. "Hmm, G2 reports the attackers as large muscular men with weird faces. They seemed to be almost bulletproof until the sailors and SEALs used our new plasma rounds. Henderson!"

A young boy appeared from nowhere. "Sir!"

"Have somebody go check on any unusually large purchases of Nair or other hair-removing solutions within the past week. Apparently, the werewolves are depilating themselves to hinder identification and confuse the issue. However, if they used a credit card, we might be able to trace the owner in time."

"Aye, and don't bother," said Donaher.

Gordon and Withers stared at him.

"Five will get you ten that the stuff was bought on cards taken from the corpses outside Hadleyville."

"You could be correct, Father," the chief admitted. "But it never hurts to check."

"On it, chief," said the lad, and he was gone. Poof.

Running a hand over his crew cut, Gordon turned to stare at the ready boards on the four walls. Red lights pinpointed the city in a dozen locations showing the presence of a firefight or mysterious explosion. Normally didn't have too many of those here. This wasn't New York.

"Damn, but the Scion is good," Horace acknowledged. "Damn good."

"So we just have to be better," added the boss softly.

Amen to that.

"Alert," calmly announced a woman gesturing over her crystal ball. The medium was in a white turban and flowing burnoose in Niagara pattern. And I do mean flowing. I could hear the water splash. "Somebody is beginning a spell of Summoning in East Cicero."

It was amazing that she was getting anything on the ball. Took a medium a long time to establish the proper reports with the mystical crystal. And these had just been teleported in from our sister organizations around the world: the Farm in England, Sunshine in Israel, the Sons of Van Helsing in United Germany, Fantasmique in France, Wally's Spook Club in Australia, etc.

Gordon raised his wrist and spoke into his watch. It was larger than ours, more complex than ours, with a teeny-weeny TV screen and a printer. But then, he was the boss.

"Roger's Rangers, there's a code three in East Cicero. Get the coordinates from Henderson."

"Anytime, anywhere, *mon Capitaine*," said the watch in stereo.

The group in the corner disappeared.

"Alert," called out another type of communications specialist at a control board. "FBI and the State Police are currently in hot pursuit of a tanker truck that has smashed through the barrier around the water purification plant in Joliet. Army has sent a flight of Apache helicopters to assist. Air Force Foxbats and Navy Tomcats are on route."

"Pierpont!" snapped Gordon.

A bald man glanced from a radar console. "Sir?"

"Watch that tanker. If it gets to within a hundred meters of the purification plant, have Finkelstein use some of our reserve magic and Gate it to the Moon."

"Sir?" chorused the whole room.

Suddenly, Horace was very embarrassed. Damn well should be. Gate the werewolves to the Moon?

"I meant that figuratively," corrected out commander in chief. "Cast it into the sun."

"Acknowledged!"

"There's been an incident at the Grand Avenue ASPCA," announced a technician holding a receiver to his ear. "Every dog and cat is gone."

The screen on his board showed a detailed vector graphic of the downtown street corner. Interesting. The Bureau hadn't used combined technology and magic since the Atlantis incident. But I guess this was the time to pull out the stops.

"Yes, yes, I know," growled Gordon impatiently. He sat and a chair appeared underneath him. "It's just the Fringeworthy doing a preemptive strike."

I couldn't stop myself. "Who, sir?"

He glared at me. "Beyond your security clearance, Ed."

Did such a thing exist? Bummer.

Tugging on the brim of his fedora, J. P. Withers lowered his hat to the floor and was gone.

"Alert!" called out a crystal ball gazer. "SAC HQ has ID'd a UFO high above I-80. DC has NG'd a TNT ICBM, but OK'd a BZ-loaded SAM to KO the UFO."

"Acknowledged," snapped Gordon, loosening his collar.

"What the hell was that?" asked Mindy.

George got a sly expression. "Oh, just an initial report."

I reached for my gun. Jessica restrained me.

"Later," I threatened.

Renault blew a kiss.

The centaur trotted close and stopped this time. "Sir, the King of the Sewers announces that all is normal in his domain."

"Thank His Majesty for me, and ask him to please continue surveillance of the underworld."

"Yes, sir."

"Shaddup!" I barked at everybody.

Although my brain was revving furiously, in some distant section of my mind I could vaguely discern that although Gordon was shocked at the behavior, he accepted it.

"Okay, what is it, Alvarez?" There was the unspoken promise that it better be good, or I'd be guarding the fuzzy dice stands at monster truck rallies for the rest of my life.

"When we fought the Scion years ago in New York, and just recently in Ohio, they used Mack trucks or tractor-trailer assemblies to haul weapons around."

"If you got a point, make it," he said, crumbling a sheet of paper and tossing it into a wastebasket, where it flared into ash.

"The Chicago underground," I said succinctly.

Faces cleared in understanding. When the City Council of 1871 was rebuilding Chicago after the great fire, they had a brilliant idea. The underground. Not to be confused with the underworld, of which we had more than enough, thank you. Summarily, it was decreed that trucks would not be allowed in downtown Chicago anymore. But in order that business could get their shipments, a subterranean copy of the main streets was built, so the trucks could deliver their goods directly to the basement of a building or store.

However, since the trucking level was poorly illuminated at night and very isolated with few easy exits, the underworld was tailor-made for the Scion. Simply drive in a few hundred truckloads of explosives and blow the city up.

Horace Gordon rubbed his chin. "Damnation, you could be right, Edwardo. ThunderBunnies!"

"Sir!" purred a vision of loveliness, loading a clip into an M-35 mini-rocket launcher.

"Go check the undercity. I'll send along a dozen or so black-white and a squad of Green Berets to assist. The ID code is 'Krakatoa.' Response: 'Vesuvius.' "

A dimple. "Gotcha, sugar."

"Sir," I objected, "Team Tunafish is perfectly ready and able to—"

"Have a rest," interrupted the chief. "The Bunnies are gone already. You've been on this from the start. Take the next hot spot."

"Alert," called out a voice. "There has been a perimeter breach at the Commonwealth Edison nuclear power station."

"A China syndrome," growled Renault, slamming a fresh clip into his Colt .45.

The dreaded China syndrome scenario. A terrorist attempt to force a meltdown at the local nuclear reactor and smother Chicago in a deadly cloud of radioactive steam. Yeah, sounded like something the Scion would go nuts over. Almost as good as nuking us directly or poisoning the water supply. Thank God this wasn't Denver with a hundred billion gallons of Hoover Dam looming overhead.

"Henderson!" bellowed Gordon. "Who do we have on ready status?"

"Nobody, sir," answered the young man from behind a chattering telex machine hard-wired to a crystal ball. Hey, maybe that was how Wall Street stockbrokers controlled the market. "Maccabees are out handling a disturbance at the City Armory, Angels are investigating a massive influx of burglar alarms at the Museum of Science and Industry."

Horace grunted. "Accepted. Tunafish, get!"

So much for our break. Hastily, we gathered supplies and I felt the first cold rush of adrenaline with the prospect of battle. Yet as I shouldered the massive Barrett, I got a gut instinct feeling that the attack on the museum was actually a greater threat to Chicago than the possible nuclear meltdown.

How is that possible? asked Jessica.

Neither mind nor gut knew. Could another piece to the

puzzle of the Scion have just dropped in our laps and we were too busy to see it? What could the Scion of the Silver Dagger possibly want in the museum? On the other hand, what couldn't you do with a warehouse full of technology and information?

Hmm.

Hmm.

13

An express elevator reserved for Bureau teams took us down twelve hundred feet to the parking garage in the subbasement. Moving fast, we chose an El Dorado stretch limousine: eight tons of armor plate and bulletproof windows. Painted a nonreflective dead black with all of the chrome removed, while not quite as impressive as our old RV, the luxury car would blend into the surroundings better.

Stay low and keep moving, that was my motto for the month.

A huge pentagram had been spray-painted on the corrugated steel of the garage door. As we approached, the design shimmered into a picture of the Eisenhower turnpike. With me at the wheel, we raced into the magical gateway, neatly merging with westbound traffic. I don't think anybody even noticed us.

At ninety miles per hour, we crashed through the flimsy toll barrier and rocketed along a secondary street, wildly zigzagging through traffic. We had wanted to teleport directly to the nuclear power station, but apparently defensive wards had been cast around the place, sealing it off from intrusion. Our mages were trying to batter down the mystical jamming, but in the meantime we readied our weapons and put the pedal to the metal.

Taking another side road, we hurtled into the country. Farms and crops gave way to weeds and forest. A few miles later, the limo moved past the minor obstruction of some yellow rubber cones and we found ourselves facing a more formidable barrier of a roaring assortment of construction equipment: dump trucks, steamrollers, graders, mixers, generators and the supremely important coffee wagon.

I slowed at the approach of a large burly woman in faded

denims, a sweaty work shirt and an unbreakable plastic yellow hard hat. However, there was a suspicious bulge by her right ankle, almost exactly the correct shape and position for a .22 automatic pistol. The preferred weapon for undercover police officers.

"Road's closed, mack," she yelled. "You got to circle round and take Hinkle Road."

I brought the limo to a halt and exchanged smiles with Jessica. It was a good lie. There was no such street as Hinkle and you couldn't circle round. Just trying would get anybody hopelessly lost. Which should deter any sane person, maybe even news reporters. But then I noticed the nervous look on many of the operators and that two had fresh bandages on throat and leg.

The Scion had been here.

As the annoyed foreperson stopped outside my door, I gave the woman a fast once-over with my sunglasses. Through the Kirlian-sensitive lenses I could see that her aura was human. The matter had never really been in doubt, but when on assignment, it's better to take nothing for granted.

With fingertip pressure, I hit the button to lower the slab of Armorlite which served us as a window.

She frowned. "Hey, jerk. I told you—"

"Cerberus," I said.

A pause. "Horatio."

"Balder."

Nodding, the foreman placed two fingers into her mouth and gave a sharp whistle. In ragged harmony, the motors of the trucks and graders started with a roar and dutifully parted to form a slim passageway between their amassed tonnage. Taking it slow, I eased the limo through the leviathan gauntlet and moved on down the road.

A few miles later was a squad of State Police cars in a standard broken H pattern blocking the road. Maybe fifty cops were present, a good dozen of them in full SWAT uniforms of flak jackets and combat helmets and holding M-16 rifles. Even the K9 Corps was present, hard-muscled German shepherds walking in tight formation at the heels of their human partners. Wooden sawhorses adorned with

lashing red lights completed the ensemble of authority.
There was a bomb disposal truck and a waiting ambulance.

And off on the berm were four smashed police cars that
esembled the losers in a demolition derby. One had win-
lows coated with something red. I decided not to look too
closely.

Stepping in the middle of the roadway, a ton of muscle in
a state trooper's uniform held out a palm to stop our approach. The other hand rested ominously on the scarred butt
of his HK 9mm. Lowering the window, I extended an arm
through the opening to display my commission booklet.

He was properly unimpressed. "Thanks for coming, but
we already captured the escaped prisoners."

"Cerberus," I stated impatiently.

His eyes narrowed. "Horatio."

"Balder."

There was a pause and he moved towards the HK.

"Right," I hastily added, and he relaxed. Whew. Different
checkpoints, different codes.

Removing his hand from the proximity of his gun, the officer took the mike from his shoulder rest and chatted for a
few seconds. Three of the four cars in the H moved out of
our way. In passing it was plain that the fourth would never
go anywhere again except the junkyard.

"What hit these guys?" asked George, frowning.

Jessica was vague. "Somewhere between forty and fifty
enemy troops in bulletproof fur coats."

"Bulletproof!" admonished Father Donaher. "But . . . you
mean the new plasma bullets didn't stop the werewolves?"

Holding the amulet of her necklace, Jessica listened to secret thoughts. "The rounds haven't arrived yet. Too many
delivery points and only so many people who can be spared
to do the task."

"Swell," I muttered. "Just swell."

The road went serpentine for a mile, probably a landscap-
ing ruse to help hide the evil power plant from rabid environ-
mentalists, and then straightened. Now facing us were four
mammoth Abrams tanks, their gigantic 120mm cannons
lowered to exactly car height. The colossal military ma-

chines were backed by mobile artillery, TOW missil
launchers, howitzers with crates of linked 40mm shell
standing open and ready for immediate use, .50 machin
guns, bazooka teams, Bradley assault vehicles and dozens o
Hummers with stanchion-mounted 40mm electric mini
guns.

I hit the brakes.

Wounded troops were everywhere. Stumbling towards th
waiting medical choppers with the help of a friend or lyin
on stretchers and moaning in pain. Spent shell casing cov
ered the ground like brass snow, and the charred wreckage o
two Apache helicopters lay partially hidden in the weeds.

Bright light bobbed in the sky as fully mobile gunship
traveled low and steady along the outer perimeters of th
barricade. Whew. On both sides of the roadway, the trees an
weedy bushes were filled with glittering strings of concer
tina wire. Miles of it. Nearby was a flatbed trailer truck half
filled with the plastic boxes the deadly stuff came packed i
and drums of the chemical compound used to dissolve th
wire. Not ecologically sound, but neat and fast.

George gave a whistle. "They've got enough concertina t
encircle the whole damn plant."

"Twice!" added Blanco, face against the Armorlite glass

"It didn't help," said Jessica in a small voice.

Just then a squirrel scampered out of the bushes and en
tered the clear band of burned-off grass. A guard shouted
Others turned. And the arboreal rodent was hit with machin
guns and grenades, and then the deafening roar of a
Atchinson rapid-fire machine shotgun vomited a storm o
lead and steel. As the smoke cleared, a team of soldiers i
silvery chemical warfare suits moved in to cleanse the are
with flamethrowers.

I heartily approved. The official orders were that nothin
goes in, or out, without proper authorization. I was please
to see the troops so literal in their compliance.

At our approach, a middle-aged man turned around fron
the group of bedraggled soldiers examining an M-16 with
barrel bent like a pretzel. The general was a big man, com
pletely filling the combat green-black uniform of the 157t

Illinois Regulars. The brim of his web-covered helmet was mathematically straight, shoes mirror-polished, pants sharply creased, and at his belt holster, instead of the standard Colt .45 automatic, was a mammoth blue-steel Blackhawk .44 AutoMag. A nasty weapon suitable for killing rogue Buicks and assorted small buildings.

The two-star general glowered at us. I glowered back and he started limping over.

I glanced at Jess.

Broken leg, she sent. *He tackled a werewolf bare-handed to hold it in place so one of the Abrams could shoot the beast.*

Much as ex-Pfc George Renault disliked brass, he positively shone at the officer in admiration. No wonder he was in charge. Briefly, I wondered if he believed in magic. The Bureau could use a man like that.

"Did it work?" asked Raul curiously, leaning forward in his plush contoured seat.

"No."

Oh.

"FBI," I stated, doffing my commission booklet and flashing my badge. Dutifully, the rest of my team tried their very best to appear tough, alert and wary. The quintessential description of every federal operative in existence.

I let him have a good look at the badge and photo ID card. A bit dusty, it was my real badge. Edwardo Alvarez, FBI, Justice Department, subdivision Bureau 13. It wasn't often we got to announce the fact in public.

My badge glowed brightly as he held it, informing him that I was the real article and informing me that he was ditto.

In the distance, I could see the Commonwealth Edison power plant and faintly heard the crackle of small-arms fire. It was infuriating to just sit here, but without proper ID, these troops would do their best to blow us into atoms. And the perimeter guards were going nowhere.

After a moment, the general snorted his disdain and pushed away the proffered booklet. "Trust me, with that suit, you don't need a badge."

What? Oh yeah. I was still wearing my FBI-clone clothes.

A real plainclothes federal agent was as close to invisible as science alone could make him.

"What happened here?" I asked, sliding my commission booklet into a breast pocket so that the badge was on open display.

"Screw us!" he roared. "Get in there and frag those geeks!"

Startled, I stomped on the gas pedal and the limo lurched ahead.

The road beyond was blown to pieces. Blast craters made the stretch resemble a flat colander. I was impressed. Unable to move beyond their appointed position, the army had blasted the Scion every inch of the way as they fled.

How nice to deal with professionals.

The stout limo jounced through endless craters until we reached an eight-foot-tall triple-wire fence surrounding the place. Actually, it was three fences on top of one another. The outer two were plastic-coated, while the middle carried enough voltage to achieve the Tesla effect, if necessary. And yet torn in that formidable barrier was a hole big enough to herd elephants.

Rolling through the breach, we skirted around a flatbed truck loaded with concrete pillars. A crude but effective battering ram. Damn their efficiency!

Beyond was a chained dog run. Scattered inside were the remains of what resembled German shepherds. As there was no time, or place, to go around, I accelerated the limo and tried to ignore the meaty bumps we rolled over. Mike said a brief prayer as we passed by. Jessica looked as if she was going to be ill.

There still remained one defense for the nuclear reactor. I hoped it worked.

Straight ahead was a three-story brick building. Offices. To the north was the two-hundred-foot-tall fluted ceramic structure of the cooling tower. It was what people saw wafting into the sky as they hastily drove past a nuke power plant. Geez, it was only warm water vapors, about as harmful as . . . ah, steam. To the south was an encased area filled with power transformers directly connected to an array of metal skeleton towers, the high-voltage transmission lines which feed the electricity into town.

And in the midst of this stone and steel grandeur, dominating the landscape, was a huge smooth concrete dome. The emergency containment vessel. Resembling an inverted granite soup bowl, it completely covered the main reactor building, so that in case of a core meltdown, the cloud of radioactive steam couldn't escape.

What about Chernobyl?

The Russians had tried to save money on the plant and didn't bother to erect a containment vessel.

Bad move.

Yowsa.

Cars from the parking lot had been driven into a circle around the plant. The limo smashed the little things aside, as easily as the werewolves had climbed over them. Beyond was a collection of broken sawhorses that had once offered meager defiance to the adamantine beasts. But no human corpses, as there wasn't a living soul in the whole complex. Had the hairy beasties noticed?

The front doors had been locked, and the handles linked together with plastic shipping straps, tough as leather. But the plastic had been snapped like taffy, and the doors completely ripped free from the thick alloy casing frames.

Could even a werewolf do that?

Gingerly, we stepped through the shattered windows, wary of the jagged glass daggers ringing our entrance. Inside, the whole lobby was blackened by fire, and charred lumps of meat announced that a few of the Scion had died from the land mines hidden under the plush carpet. Turnabout was fair play.

Three hallways branched out from the lobby, one blocked with office furniture in a crude barricade. Mindy was already at the hallway, prodding the furniture scraps with her sword. I checked the wall map, mindful of the intentional errors in it. "Yep, the reactor is this way."

A lumpy shape blotted the floor in shadow.

"Twelve o'clock high!" I cried, firing a Magnum at the overhead lights.

In a spray of broken tiles, a huge creature dropped from the ceiling to bounce off the receptionist's desk and land atop a decorative glass table—which instantly shattered beneath the impact of the heavy being, slashing its scaled legs to ribbons.

Ha! I always knew those things were dangerous.

Scaled? It was a gargoyle.

As the snarling beast struggled to free itself from the ruin of the table, Jessica's machine pistol sprayed a deadly combo of lead, steel and the new plasma rounds at the animated monster. Annoyed, the beast hissed its defiance and vomited a stream of acid-based enzymes. A golden ray from Raul's wand diverted the stream in midair. The poison hit a computer terminal, which began dissolving. An arrow from Mindy bounced off an eye of the gargoyle. Donaher hosed the beast with liquid fire. Tina shackled its mouth shut.

With a fiendish grin, George snicked off the safety of his Masterson assault cannon and started pounding the living stone-beast with armor-piercing HE rounds. Slammed into the plastic mock-up of the nuclear furnace, the gargoyle was held motionless under the furious onslaught of caseless HE. A perfect target.

Holstering the .357 Magnum, I leveled the Barrett, took aim and squeezed the trigger.

At first, I thought the rifle had jammed and exploded on me. Mentally, I braced myself for the pain of my own shrapnel. Then I realized the gargoyle had no head.

"That," stated Raul firmly, pointing to the motionless statue, "is no werewolf!"

"Faith, lad, we called in friends," said Father Mike, adjusting the sizzling preburner on his weapon. "Apparently, so did they."

"But why?"

Sourly, George tapped his rifle. "What kind of ammo we carrying?"

"Silver," I answered. The light bulb clicked on. "Which will do nothing special to a non-were!" And any other ammo was miles away at the Sears Tower. Bloody marvelous.

I shouldered the massive Barrett. "That was just a guard.

Come on, I'm on point. Raul on rear. One-meter spread. Let's go!"

Hurriedly, we started down the central hallway when a siren outside began to wail. Loud enough to rattle a broken window, the steam whistle keen did not need Jessica, our universal translator, to decode its dire message.

"Meltdown," breathed Mindy.

And we smiled.

14

"Yes!" I cried, raising a clenched fist in victory.

Jessica and Mike shook hands. George and Raul did a high five. Mindy hugged Tina.

"Let's go get 'em!" shouted Renault, brandishing his M-60.

Scrambling more than running, we hurried along the central hallway. This was our big chance. Destroying the nuclear power plant was such an obvious ploy that precautions had been taken. Every city that possessed a nuke also had a full-scale working model of the plant in which to train new personnel. It was an exact duplicate, with the proper pipes hot or cold, live steam in the turbines and a vibrating floor. Completely draining the magic from a fully charged mage, the Bureau switched the two buildings. The real power plant was a hundred feet to the west. This was the model. Perfect bait to finally capture a werewolf.

But if the Scion deduced the truth and managed to find the operating plant, Chicago could very quickly get blowtorched off the face of the Earth. A sobering thought.

The fake alarms never stopped or slowed.

Turning a corner, we faced a set of double doors with a gaping hole in the middle. The team paused when Mindy spotted a trip wire and George deactivated the claymore mine attached. Just a gift from the Scion.

Beyond those doors was another set, and then more. Finally, we reached a more formidable portal. The door was a seamless slab of highly polished alloy. There was no lock, handle, window, keypad, keyhole, card slot, sensor pad or dial. And lying on the floor was a very dead technician.

Jessica faced a corner and vomited.

The poor man had been in the wrong place at the wrong time. I took off my FBI jacket and draped it over as much of him as possible.

"Damn beasties must be on the other side of this wee door," reasoned Father Donaher, radiating anger hotter than his flamethrower.

"Okay, how do we get past this?" demanded George, panting slightly from our brisk run.

"Nobody does," I said, shifting the cushioned strap of the Barrett rifle. "Obviously, the whole plant has undergone primary lock-down!"

"Which means?" demanded Mindy, her sword in both hands, ready for action.

I thumped the armored portal. "Meaning that nobody gets in until the President personally commands the Atomic Energy Commission to send the step-down code."

"But this is only the model!" someone wailed.

"Which functions exactly as the original."

Donaher whipped out his pocket cellular phone.

Reaching out a pale hand, Jessica closed the phone. "We'd never reach the White House quickly enough."

Separated from capturing our enemies by only a meter of reactive metal alloy. It was infuriating!

In an unprecedented move, George spit the gum out of his mouth. "Okay, the front door is locked. How about a side window? Or we could do the old Santa Claus bit with a chimney flue."

"Nyet," said Blanco, her eyes glazed. A wizard's inner sight is often a wonderful thing at times. This was one of them. "Scion did not pass door."

"Eh?"

"What?"

Impulsively, I glanced around. "Then where are they?"

"Ohmigod," breathed Jessica, staring at the floor.

Although most of the dead man was covered with my darkening suit jacket, the mangled remains of his arms and legs were horribly apparent. And I did a double-take when I saw what my wife had noticed. Wholly intact, his undamaged left arm was fully outstretched, with a single finger pointing to the west.

Towards the real plant.

Yikes! Not murdered, but tortured!

George took Raul by the shoulder. "Ra, get us out of here!"

With a furious expression, the mage stomped his staff upon the floor.

Nothing happened.

Hey, the body was gone. And the meltdown alarm was strangely quiet.

"This is the real power plant!" cried Father Donaher in understanding.

Horta kissed his wand.

"Nice," I acknowledged hastily. "Mindy, carve that door to pieces!"

"No need," she said, pointing upward. "Look."

We craned our necks. There was a gaping hole in the ceiling above us, continuing for several levels. Beyond that, even with maximum augmentation from my sunglasses, I saw nothing.

Father Mike raised an eyebrow. "The defenses of the main control center were too great?"

Pulling the bolt on her Uzi machine pistol, Jessica scoffed. "No way. But if anybody tries to force entry, the whole plant shuts off with overrides. Then the Scion could never get the meltdown they want."

"But out here?" asked Tina, confused. "What can were-wolves do outside reactor?"

Yeah, what could Scion do out here? Any computer commands from the office building had to be routed through the main control booth and would be easily deleted by the technicians. No important equipment was external of the containment shell. And without computer guidance, the only place a meltdown could be forced was the main reactor.

No, *in* the main reactor.

"Merciful Heaven, they're headed straight for the core!" cried Father Donaher, almost dropping his shotgun. "Going in from above!"

"Brilliant!" I reluctantly agreed.

George was croggled. "Through the containment shell? It's ten meters thick!"

But the ploy made sense. They would encounter no real security devices or defenses on the outside of the building. Thirty meters plus of ferroconcrete to pierce and they were home free.

Faintly in the distance, I heard another explosion from the perimeter. Just another rabbit, or the Scion trying to escape after finishing the sabotage? Suddenly, a soft horn began bleating. The actual meltdown alert? Hoo boy.

Crouching low, Mindy jumped and pulled herself onto the next level. "Come on!" she cried. "It's an easy climb!"

Yeah, right.

Gesturing and chanting, Christina tapped our miscellaneaous footwear with her wand and we each raised a leg and carefully placed a shoe on the wall. With a lurch, the team lifted the other foot and now stood on the curving dome, our bodies perpendicular to the ground. In standard attack formation we raced the three stories to the roof. Flying would have been faster, but this was a magic minimum mission. How many additional battles would we have to fight tonight?

Stretching endlessly above was the containment vessel. A quarter million tons of formed, prestressed concrete reinforced with every artifice available to modern science. Spiraling around the dome was a series of dots, bare bolts indicating where the access ramp leading to the top had originally been, but removed for this emergency.

But high off to the side was a dark unidentifiable splotch. At crazy angles to the ground, we scampered forward. If the military was watching us through binoculars, somebody was asking for aspirin right about now.

The splotch was a hole.

Keeping well clear of the opening, we gathered around the breach in the concrete. The passage was roughly six feet in diameter, neat and round as if done by a shoemaker's awl. A disquieting, if picturesque, visual.

I turned my head slowly so as not to experience vertigo. "Raul, stay here on rear guard."

Horta nodded. "Natch."

"And if the worst happens, can you do a prismatic shield over the whole plant?"

The wizard made a face as if digesting a brick. "Ah . . . yeah. Maybe. If I paint runes."

Jessica handed him a crayon. "Then start drawing. If we fail, you erect a shield."

"With you guys trapped inside?"

Snapping the huge clip loose, I checked the load on the Barrett. "That's the order, Marnix."

The use of his real name shocked the mage. And after a moment, he nodded.

As we started inside, I saw Horta using the crayon to hastily write mystic symbols on the smooth concrete, take a side-step, do another, and step again. If the wizard had a whole plant to surround with those things, he'd better hurry. But then, we had better, too.

The inside of the tubular hole was silky smooth and dotted with the ends of flexible black iron bars, gray lead plates and yellowish cadmium sheeting. So far, our watches had remained silent. I pressed the test switch and was satisfied that the Geiger function was working. But if these babies started clicking, well, even magic can only heal so much. What the hey, I had a lot of friends waiting for me in Heaven, and all of my enemies were in Hell.

Stepping free, we were a meter above a metal lattice cat-walk that encircled the dome at several levels. Probably for inspections. There was a low humming noise that permeated the air and vibrated softly in the walls and floor. Below was an impossible maze of pipes, conduits, condensers and just assorted stuff. Occasionally, a hiss sounded, or a dull cluck of an automatic valve closing. The place resembled a car engine from an ant's perspective.

Marring the angular perfection of this technological jungle gym was a pattern of pipes bent or crushed aside to accommodate something much larger than human.

Yep, that was our boys. If it ain't ours, break it.

"Tina, stay here and try to repair the hole in the concrete."
She nodded and went to work. Good woman.

On point, Mindy dropped silent to the catwalk. The rest of
the team followed as best we could. Our first indication that
we were getting close was a dead technician, impaled on a
manual release wheel. Not the shaft, but the wheel itself.
Mindy scrutinized the disgusting corpse for a whole second.

"Unnecessary," she declared, and we moved on.

Soon, a grinding sound could be heard above the
hypnotizingly balanced hum of the reactor and turbines. In
the distance, partially obscured by pipes and mist, we could
see a bullet-shaped metal construct with thick conduits connected to every side. The pressure chamber of the nuclear reactor. The grinding noise was coming from a shuddering
machine held in the hairy paws of a gang of werefolk. Supported by a sling, the roaring diesel engine powered a whirling cone covered with concentric teeth. The ancient drill
bucked and shuddered as the monsters forcibly held the re-
luctant tool against the heat-slick covering of the core. Already, the outer wall of the chamber had been segmented and
pried out of the way. Chunks of thermal insulation and inter-
locking slabs of graphite lay discarded on the lattice flooring. Like a chain saw chewing wood, this mining machine
was eating a path into the final wall. Beyond that was only
superheated steam, hard radiation and certain death.

"Can't risk the flamethrower in here," said Donaher, tuck-
ing the sprayer into his belt and stroking the pump action on
his Remington. "Might finish the job for the Scion."

"And no time for finesse," stated Renault grimly. "Let's
just kill them."

Mindy gave a broad smile. "At last, a battle plan I like."

"Routine one," I agreed, leveling the mighty Barrett on a
frosty horizontal pipe. "On my mark."

In the Starlite scope, I got a clear view of the were direct-
ing the drill; then I relocated the cross hairs onto the drill itself and squeezed the trigger. *Ba-doom!*

Torn from its grip, the ruptured diesel spun away, spewing
oil as it clanged off the reactor and plummeted downward.

With slack jaws, the Scion turned and we cut loose.

The deer slugs from Father Donaher's shotgun punched a
hole in one monster big enough for Mindy to feather the one
behind him with a silver-tipped arrow. Both monsters
seemed incredibly surprised. Jessica hosed them with a
stream of 9mm Parabellums from her Uzi, and I blew a
fourth to pieces. Body armor didn't mean crap to the Barrett
and our new plasma rounds. Why hadn't I gotten one of
these sooner? Would have made a fine birthday gift.

Too difficult to wrap. Shaddup.

Although rattled by our appearance, the remaining fur-
faces rallied to the fight. Two flank weres trained their
MAC-10 machine pistols at us, sending a hail of .22 bullets
zipping our way. Meanwhile, the rest of the beasts started
stuffing blocks of a clayish material in the nearly finished
breach. It was C3, a high-explosive plastique.

I held my breath to facilitate aiming. *Ba-doom!* And a
headless werewolf jerked backwards, the fistful of detonators in her paw falling among the complex piping.

"Here!" ordered Jessica, handing a copper bracelet to
Mindy. In a blur of motion, the martial artist tied the metallic
band to an arrow with a strip of cloth, pulled, aimed, released.

Streaking past the Scion, the arrow jammed itself into the
thin strip of exposed insulation edging the puncture in the reactor casing. Grabbing her necklace, Jess stared. With a
flash, the gash was gone, and the outer shell was as smooth
and perfect as the day it was forged.

Gleefully, George triggered the Masterson.

In short controlled bursts, he sprayed the support legs of
the platform the Scion agents stood on. And with a screech
of stretching metal, the flooring tore free from its moorings
and the werefolk tumbled downward, bouncing and slamming off the maze of pipes like hairy pinballs.

"After them," I commanded, shouldering the Barrett. "We
want a captive!"

Angling off to the side, the team headed for the walkway
and stairs. There was a convenient air shaft close by, but we
ignored that. I'd fought my share of monsters in air vents
and didn't care for the experience. They had the advantage

that I was trapped, but I had the advantage that they couldn't dodge my bullets. So it equaled out. I hated that. Nothing worse than a fair fight with monsters.

"Didn't know you could trigger a spell from a distance."

If nobody is wearing the bracelet, of course.

Interesting.

An explosion sounded from below and a siren began howling.

Startled, I smacked my forehead with a palm. Idiot! The Scion, detonators and the C3 had each dropped to the ground floor. Reunited, they were back in business. Chicago wasn't safe yet.

Options came and went like cars on the freeway. Then a beauty screeched to a halt. Frantically, I looked around. Where the hell was it . . . ah!

Behind an incredibly thick window of bulletproof plastic was the reactor control room. Terrified technicians stared at us. Every inch of every wall was jammed with meters, dials, knobs and switches. A circular bank of controls fronted the status board, which showed every conceivable nuance of condition inside the core. How could anybody learn to operate this thing? It made my VCR seem simple.

"Jess, tell them to do a shutdown!"

They can't. The main computer crashed, and the auxiliary doesn't respond and they aren't leaving the control room to operate the manual overrides with those monsters running amuck.

"Then tell them to get clear!"

The men and women dropped out of sight.

Leveling the Barrett, I aimed at the distant cluster of control panels. *Ba-doom!* The shatterproof window shattered into a zillion pieces. *Ba-doom!* Pieces of electrical console sprayed into the air. Sparks crawled everywhere. *Ba-doom!*

And the muted rumble in the floor died away.

Satisfied, we moved on. It was an obscure piece of information I had once read in a scientific journal, that if the control room of a nuclear reactor received significant damage, an independent subsystem seized control of the core and did a priority shutdown. I.e., shoot it and it breaks.

Advanced technology is so primitive.

Scampering down the stairs, I kicked open a locked wire-mesh door and ducked as a ricochet went past my head. Shotgun in one hand, flamethrower in the other, Father Donaher gave suppressing cover as the team regrouped on the ground floor. We took cover behind a stack of steel drums used for who-knows-what in this place. Maybe clam dip for the boss.

Ten meters across what resembled a loading bay, the furred terrors had established a workable redoubt by ramming a forklift into a pile of pallets. Having found their MAC-10 machine pistols along with the plastique, two weres were wildly spraying us with small-caliber bullets, firing nonstop, without any consideration for ammo reserves. A good tactic that just might work. And we were at a serious disadvantage since we still didn't want to hurt the reactor behind them. Meltdown had been made impossible, but if breached, the boiling radioactive water inside the core would kill everybody here. Then again, maybe that was their new plan. Take us with them. Okay, time to get clever.

Getting her attention, I displayed three fingers to my wife and waved them around. Jess nodded and sent the message to the team.

Clutching his throat, Donaher gurgled in pain and dropped behind the barrels.

"Damn!" I cried real loud. "My gun is jammed!"

"I'm out of bullets!" added Mindy.

"My leg!" gasped Jessica, kneeling expectantly.

Grinning like fiends, the werewolves charged.

Shmucks.

Still somewhere in the rafters above, George cut loose with the Masterson assault cannon, angling his shots to make damn sure he did not hit the reactor shell.

Their bodies jerking wildly, the Scion agents did a little dance of death as the silver-tipped mini-shells blew them to hell in nine pieces. Jessica did mop-up with the Uzi, Donaher set them on fire, Mindy cut off everybody's head with her sword and my Magnums blasted anything that seemed healthy or hairy. No sense wasting the Barrett on dead fish in a barrel.

"Die!" Jessica cried, holding her glowing necklace, and empty air filled with a dead werewolf turning visible.

Amazing. How had she found him?

Bad breath.

Lack of flossing saves America. Film at eleven.

Black blood dripping off a flaming paw, the largest were-wolf pulled a small velvet bag from his tattered flak jacket and tossed it at us. We braced for an explosion, but nothing happened.

The team pointed an arsenal his way.

"Alive for questioning!" I cried.

Reluctantly, the weapons dropped.

"Sic . . . 'em . . . ," he commanded, and then died.

Sic 'em?

Expanding, the velvet bag tore apart as out stepped one mother-ugly monster: fifteen feet tall, with four skinny legs, six muscular arms and a bulbous head made entirely of ten-tacles lined with suckers filled with teeth, and tipped with taloned claws.

A weresquid? Would silver kill a weresquid?

Shoot it and see.

I placed my last four shots from the Barrett into the pulsa-ting chest of this thing and I'm not sure it noticed. Okay, sil-ver meant bupkis to the Wiggling Wonder.

Stepping in close, Father Mike butt-stroked the beast in the face with the wooden stock of his shotgun. Wood af-fected a lot of supernaturals. A whipping tentacle slammed the big priest aside to crash into a tool locker. Donaher went limp on the floor, blood flowing from his face. A no go on the wood, then.

Her wrist jerked and Mindy buried a knife into its body. Then she added a couple of throwing stars. *Nada.* Jessica peppered it with assorted 9mm rounds, but lead, steel, wood, silver and phosphorus had no noticeable effect, except maybe to slow it down a bit with all that weighty metal tucked inside.

"Cadillac Seville!" warned George, flipping the Masterson to full auto. But the fiery stream of shells merely vanished into the body of the weird aquatic beast.

Scrambling to the moaning priest, I pulled open his cassock. Strapped around his chest was a bulky vest made completely of pockets, each numbered and containing a shotgun shell. Since we were fighting werecreatures, Donaher had requisitioned a full bane collection. Good move.

These shells did not contain lead pellets or steel shot, but every known type of natural substance which had a negative effect on evil supernaturals: wolfsbane leaves, dragonsbane bark, salt, silver filings, garlic powder, thorns from a wild white rose, sawdust, mandrake root, minced bat wing, dried dodo droppings, essence of newt, powdered thulium, shredded income tax forms and instant coffee. The real stuff. Decaf didn't do nothing to nobody.

Mindy cut off a tentacle. The bodiless limb wrapped itself around her torso and started to squeeze.

In a flat pocket was a tiny booklet and I fast read the enclosed bane chart: shrew, skunk, shriner—oh hell, octopus was the closest we had to a squid. Was an octopus a relative of a squid? What was a squid anyway? A mollusk? Isn't that in the clam family? Only one way to find out.

Flamboyantly pulling the pin with his teeth, George threw a thermite grenade at the wiggling monstrosity. It caught the sphere in a tentacle and threw the grenade back. Renault dove out of the way and a time clock was engulfed in searing flames. No loss.

Then the water sprinklers came on, a fire bell started clanging and a calm voice began telling us to run, not walk, to the nearest exit.

Dripping wet, I frantically rummaged through the mess of shells until I found the huckleberry-bush ash picked by a left-handed virgin and burned on an even day of the week.

Avoiding a whipping tentacle, Jessica dropped her Uzi, but recovered to taser the thing in a leg. Nothing.

I thumbed in the only anti-wereclam shell we had, turned and triggered the weapon. As the gun exploded, the beast screamed in pain and began clawing at the bloody ruin of its mighty chest. Yes! The solo tentacle dropped off a gasping

Mindy, and in ragged stages the beast collapsed to the ground. Slowly, its form softened, blurred and re-formed into a . . . little . . . tiny . . . goldfish?

I dropped the gun. What the hell was this? Some kind of demented joke? Taking inventory of the enemy, I could only gasp when I saw they were dogs and cats. None of them were human. Then the answer came to me like a fist in the dark.

We had been tricked!

And the clock went *tick*.

15

Quickly, I recovered my aplomb. "Jess, call in Raul and Tina! George, check Donaher. Mindy on guard." They moved.

Grabbing hold of the amulet around her neck, Jess scrunched in concentration and with a flash the mages appeared. Wands sparking, the wizards searched for danger.

I snapped fingers for attention. "Ra, I need HQ now. Full contact."

"Why-o-mino, pal-o-mino?" asked Horta.

"Do it!"

The mage grunted. Marking a spot in the air with the glowing tip of his wand, Raul drew a floating square. Chanting under her breath, Tina reached out to twist a bit of nothingness, and with a loud click the phosphorescent square formed into a view of the War Room with Horace Gordon shouting orders to people. Neat! I wondered if we could get free HBO this way.

"Hello, Mountaintop," I reported. "This is Manhattan Project. We've been tricked! These aren't the genuine articles, but cheap copies!"

"Copies? You sure, Alvarez?" demanded the boss. One second later, his image mouthed the same words. Little time lag here. In the background, some bedraggled ThunderBunnies were donning fresh clothing and the wall maps were blinking with warning lights.

"These perps are not humans," I reported furiously, "but animals bitten and turned into werecreatures!"

"Then why was the goldfish in a bag?" asked Renault, pouring a Healing potion over Father Donaher.

Mindy grunted. "Heck, magic can only up your IQ so far. Dogs and cats are naturally smart. Any angler knows that fish are only animated vegetables."

"Too true."

Horace Gordon rubbed a hoary hand across a grizzled chin.

"Animal agents, eh? The crafty bastards."

I heartily agreed. "These attacks have only been a diversion to keep us from . . ." And there my line of reasoning ran out of steam. To keep us from doing what? Where? There had to be a method to this madness. So where are the real Scion members, the mage, and that blasted telepath!

Tick-tick: 10:45 P.M.

"Sir," asked Tina, giving a curtsy. "What was at museum?"

"Um? Oh, yes. The robbers were more were-animals and some hired guns from Wisconsin."

I whistled. The best mercenaries were always ex-farmers. Strong, diligent and with incredible patience.

"What were they after?" asked Raul pensively.

"The geological exhibit," answered a petite blonde, strapping on a fresh bandolier of ammo clips. "Weird, huh?"

And the last piece of the puzzle fell into place.

"The moonrock!" George and Henderson cried together.

Understanding brightened everybody's face. It was begining to make sense now. In a never-ending quest to stir interest in space exploration, NASA would happily place on display at any public event one of their precious moonrocks.

Desperate for new personnel, the Scion had held an occult convention to try and recruit people. As an exhibit, they had gotten a moonrock. It was from another planet, high mystical energy there. But during the con, some poor werewolf had walked into a room to find itself in the direct physical presence of the Lunar Master. An event unprecedented in world history.

Which resulted in the ethereal explosion!

Damn straight. Surviving the blast, Scion members were

transformed into intelligent werewolves—their big chance to destroy the world.

"Henderson!" barked Gordon.

The young man saluted. "Sir?"

"Get that frigging rock out of the museum pronto! Take Team Angel, a company of soldiers, some police, and the Air Force Rangers."

"Done!" cried the man, and he went offscreen.

"So what we have to do is find the person holding the moonrock?" asked Mindy, chewing on a thumb. "If we break contact between this person and the moonrock, everyone becomes human again?"

Blanco shook her head. "*Nyet!* Change permanent is."

George helped Donaher to stand. The molehill and the mountain.

"Doesn't every moonrock exhibit have a radio transponder hidden in the base of its display stand, so if somebody steals the rock, NASA can find the thieves and get the moon junior back?" asked the big Irishman.

That's my priest. Always thinking.

Hands clasped behind his back, Gordon turned expectantly.

"Accessing NASA files," calmly announced a technician as he typed madly at a control console. "Transmission codes . . . frequencies . . . triangulating with New York and St. Louis . . . Got them! We've detected a radar anomaly sixty thousand feet over Peoria." Hand touched the earphone. "Our NORAD liaison reports that the anomaly vaguely resembles . . . a building?"

A flying building?

"It's the Hadleyville Hotel!" declared Henderson in delight.

Wow. Talk about a mobile headquarters. It probably held every big weapon they owned *and* the two thousand plus members. This was bad. If necessary, they could always just drop in on dowtown. Take out a couple of city blocks at least.

"This was a short war." The chief smiled. I don't remember him ever doing that before. "It doesn't matter how heavily that building may be fortified, it can't be very nimble. Plus, we now know where their mage is. Inside, keeping it aloft."

He turned. "Schwartz! Manchilde! Have our naval shore batteries launch everything they have and blow that thing out of the sky."

"Aye, sir!"

A dozen mages screamed no at the same time.

"Why?" demanded Gordon angrily.

"Because of the Death factor!" Raul stated, as if that clarified everything.

"Lord Almighty," whispered a pale ThunderBunny. "The Death Trauma factor!"

"What's that?" asked Mindy, before I could.

Blanco haltingly explained. If the werewolf holding the moonrock was violently killed, the trauma of its own death could rekindle the initial reaction.

I took over. "Converting everybody in the Chicago area into werecreatures?"

"If the hotel was close enough. Yes."

Instantly creating four million more weres. Eek.

"Four million angry, intelligent downtown werewolves," corrected Renault. "Ed, there ain't that many silver bullets in existence!"

"The end of the world," breathed Jessica.

"At least the end of humanity as the top link on the food chain," added Mindy.

Raul gave her an eloquent elbow in the ribs.

So this had been their plan from the start. The Scion would be delighted if the Bureau shot down that hotel. And if we didn't, they would drop it on Chicago with the same end result. We lose.

An engineer poked his head around the corner of the nuclear reactor. Goggle-eyed, he stared at the magic window. With a glance, Jessica sent him scurrying away.

"If the hotel is flying, why don't we add a few more Fly spells and hurtle it into space?" suggested a passing centaur, bouncing along. Geez, buy some underwear, pal.

Horace gave the matter due consideration.

"Wouldn't work," he declared. "The moment we started to augment their spell, the Scion would cancel it completely, and the hotel would immediately crash."

"And I bet they're not traveling in a straight line to Chicago," postulated Renault. "But in fact zigzagging across the country going from one population center to another."

"Safeguarding their approach."

"Exactly."

It was good military strategy. Once more we were forcibly reminded that ruthless and amoral did not equate with stupidity. And even if we shot them down over Rockville or Sheboygan, we'd still get a hundred thousand werewolves.

Although Sheboygan was an option.

Horace started pacing. "What we need is an infiltration team to get inside the hotel and rescue the werewolf with the rock." He said it calmly, as ordering a cheese sandwich. "But as this also may be a diversion, I'm sending only one team. Any volunteers?"

Hands, wings and mandibles filled the room.

Thoughtfully, Horace gazed over his cornucopia of suicides.

"Alvarez, your team is furthest west, thus the closest, and minutes count. Go stop that hotel."

Whee! Fun time. "Mission limitations?" I asked aloud.

"You have until O'Hare. The population density there is relatively thin. When the hotel reaches that point, we destroy it, even if you're still inside."

That was only to be expected.

"Plus, I will have NORAD prepare for a nuclear accident to occur at the airport to handle any residual werewolves created."

Fluttering into view, a fairy seemed perturbed. "Sir, won't the radioactive fallout from even a low-yield atomic blast

pollute Lake Michigan, contaminating half the water table of
the nation?"

"We'll have to chance it," replied the chief gruffly. "I'd
love to use a gas vapor bomb, but the prevailing winds are
too strong."

George nodded in comprehension.

"What's a gas vapor bomb?" Donaher asked *sotto voce*.

I waved him aside. "Tell you later."

"Alert," announced a woman at a crystal ball. "A group
of werewolves is attempting to open the gates of lower
Hell."

"Send J.P.!" snapped Gordon. "Tunafish, you have your
orders! Get going! " And the window went blank.

With a pass of her hand, Tina dissolved the empty square.

"Conference!" I called, and they gathered close. "Okay,
how do we get there?"

"Teleport?"

"Never seen the inside."

"Gate?"

"Can't get a psionic lock."

"Grow wings and fly?"

"For this many people? It would drain us of magic."

"Use helicopter gunships?"

"From the army outside?"

"Now, that's a good idea!"

"I like it."

"Gotta stop off at the limo first," declared Renault. "To—

And we were standing on the main access road, next to the
limo, surrounded by military personnel.

"—get more ammunition," George finished lamely. He
scowled at Horta. "Enjoy doing that, don't you?"

"Who? Me?"

"The choppers are on the way," said Jess, hand on necklace. Unlocking the trunk, I grabbed a satchel charge and
slammed a fresh clip into the Barrett.

We had a reservation at the Hadleyville Hotel.

In five minutes we were airborne.

Resembling a hatchet blade with short wings, Apache

helicopters were amazingly quiet. Sleek and fast, the trim military gunships could do a ground speed of 300 mph, had more surveillance equipment than our old RV, were radar-resistant, had a low infrared signature, were armor-proof to a 40mm shell and carried a 20mm electric machine gun in the nose. The stubby wings, unnecessary for flying, were there only to offer more room to carry weapons. My kind of transportation.

Unfortunately, the Apaches could only carry one passenger, two if we squeezed tight and sat on each other's lap, so the team had to split into four groups. Big on bottom, little on top. I got Jessica, thankfully. Tina got George, Raul got Mindy, and Donaher was the cheese.

What?

He rides alone.

Ah.

Stuffed into the front gunner's seat, Jess and I had three windows to look out, rectangular in front and trapezoidal on the sides. I could only assume there was some intelligent reason for the design, as the military was not big on esthetics. A triptych of video monitors topped a complex control panel spanning the cockpit. The middle showed a perfectly illuminated view of the ground below, the left behind us, and the right above.

Cold and clear, the dark sky was full of twinkling stars. Flying in close battle formation, we could see the other three squat choppers moving swift and silent. Maybe not properly invisible, but damn close. Rapidly, we hurtled past the sparkling lights of O'Hare Airport and into the flat Illinois farmland.

The point of no return.

"How we doing?" I said to the microphone built into the control panel. The switches and dials were marked with abbreviated phrases such as SygNob, RetVap and TacOing, so we weren't touching anything!

The pilot was aft, in a raised secondary cabin, completely sealed off from us. Both pilot and gunner could fly and shoot

he craft. If one got wounded, the other took over. Plus, in an
emergency situation, they could place the ship on autopilot
and both cut loose with the weapons system. It was an effective combination. Just ask Iraq.

"Doing fine," said the speaker in smooth undistorted
tones. "Fuel good, all systems green and according to the
navigational coordinates I'm receiving from ChiTacOp,
we'll be within strike range in ten minutes. How are you two
sardines surviving?"

"It's hard," said Jessica with a wiggle, "but we'll man-
age."

I pinched her. Stop that! This is business.

*Tee-hee. Oh, Mr. Alvarez, what a big gun you have! How
many times can it shoot?*

Sexual tension often ran high prior to battle. It was one of
the nicer perks of this job.

"We have contact," said the speaker. "I'm putting it on radar."

Removing Jessica's shoulder from my nose, I brushed
aside her long hair and saw that the middle monitor was
showing a vector graphic of the landscape moving below us.
The luminescent green radar arm swept steadily about on a
perfectly clear screen.

"See it? Sector four, mark ten degrees."

"I'll have to take your word on it," I admitted. Guess this
takes a trained eye to operate.

And a lot of quarters.

"Sheridan, this is Patton," crackled the speaker. "We have
a confirm with Craig and Schwarzkopf on our bogey."

It's the other helicopters.

"Thank you, dear," I sneered. "Now, who's Craig?"

A mental shrug.

"Roger the confirm, Patton," spoke our guy. "We are ap-
proaching go zone. Interlock guide beacons, assume formation Q and begin primary countdown."

Jessica and I scrambled to finish tying weapons to our
body harnesses. Geez, things move so fast in the Army Air
Corps.

"Ready . . . ," said the pilot in soothing tones, "set . . . and go-go-go!"

He hit the ejector button, the door slammed aside, there was a bang under our seat and we were thrown clear of the deadly flashing rotors.

Sans parachutes, my team fell through the black sky.

16

The wind whistled past our ears, but before we even had a chance to activate our Fly bracelets, the team hit velvet steel with stunning force. *Urmph!*

I shook my head to reboot my brain. Above in the starry sky, the black outlines of the Apache choppers were dwindling into the distance. Below was the landscape moving at a steady progression, and around me was the moaning team lying on air.

Okay, we knew the hotel was invisible. But even after we landed on it? Good spell.

We haven't hit it yet.

"We're not on the roof?" asked Donaher, arms and legs splayed as if in free fall.

Sitting upright, Raul stared at him. "Does it frigging feel like we're on the roof? This is a prismatic sphere! A kind of forceshield, magical bubble around the hotel."

Our daredevil Jennings was standing on the sky.

Why did I arrest her, your honor? No visible means of support.

Shaddup.

"How do we get through?" asked Mindy, oblivious to my private conversation with Jess.

"Ask Tina!"

I stared at our Russian mage. Blanco was waving fingers, weaving trails of light and studying the results.

"Runes of defense!" she barked at last.

We waited for explanations.

Tick . . . tick . . .

"Runes of defense, or defensive runes?" demanded Raul. I guess this particular branch of magic was her specialty.

"What's the difference?" I demanded back at him.

"One cancels the effect of offensive weapons, but the other only repels the very physical presence of enemies to the caster."

"So one rune keeps out the weapon," rationalized Mindy, "but the other holds off the people?"

"Yep."

"Defensive runes!" cried Tina.

George popped a stick of gum into his mouth. "Which?"

"Weapons!"

"Then people can get in?"

"Long as we don't have any weapons," she declared. "And don't try to hurt the building!"

Good enough.

"Dump 'em!" I shouted, tossing my Magnums away. Hell, we didn't even have a coded battle phrase for this contingency. When had it ever been necessary for us to get rid of weapons?

Slowly, reluctantly, the team began to disarm.

The Barrett slid over an invisible hump and tumbled into the night. Satchel charge, grenades, signet ring, cigarette lighter, trick pens. I still wasn't going through. Ah, in my ankle holster was a Bureau derringer. And my pocketknife. And the Swiss Army knife . . .

Father Donaher's flamethrower vanished like a lead safe, along with his shotgun, bane vest, wristwatch, pocketknife, pens, rosary garrote, and holy-water pistol. Smoothly, he sank out of sight. But then, priests travel light.

Jess dumped her taser, Uzi, ammo clips, grenades, pocket camera, watch, a couple of loaded hypodermic needles from her medical kit, two earrings, an inflatable pentagram, some pens, Swiss Army knife and two bracelets.

Bracelets! That's why I hadn't gone through yet.

Stoically, Renault slapped and twisted the release buckle on his chest harness. Straps whipping wildly, the Masterson flew off.

Now, that was going to cause damage when it hit ground. Boy, I sure hope we weren't over a playground or anything.

Renault added the ammo belt, the Colt .45, a derringer,

two knives, a switchblade, his wristwatch, some pens, brass knuckles and his hat.

His hat?

"Ed, I . . . I can't do it," cried Mindy, tears running down her cheeks. She was hugging the scabbard of her sword with both arms.

Crap! This was an unforeseen development. Jennings release that sword? She had spent ten years of her life on a physical and spiritual quest to obtain the blade. I once saw her dive into a lake of boiling water just to retrieve the scabbard. Whatever the bond was between sword and woman, it went beyond the boundaries of such mundane considerations as sanity and common sense.

I waved at her. "It's okay, Min. Everybody has limitations. Fly off and rendezvous with the choppers. Act as a relay and direct their actions if necessary."

Wordless, she nodded and drifted away on the winds.

Stripped naked; and we just lost our best bare-knuckle fighter. Some invasion force we were.

"Hey, how about you guys?" I shouted over the wind.

Raul snapped at me. "We're discussing it!"

Discussing what?

Who stays and who guards the other person's staff.

Aw crap, a mage also?

Tick . . . tick . . .

With a stone face, Christina Blanco gave her staff to Raul. She tossed off her vest, a Swiss Army knife, some vials of potions, a bundle of envelopes containing powders, the bandolier of wands, a pair of velvet gloves and more bracelets than I could easily count. Tina still wasn't passing, until she pulled down her jacket, exposing her shoulder, and her butterfly took to the winds.

The tattoo? Well, I guess it was offensive to purists.

Okay. Better strip ship. I threw behind my wristwatch, another speedloader for the Magnums, the Lightning Blast bracelet, the Disintegrate and the Flame Lance. This left me with Fly, Jump Start and Teleport. Still here. I added my burglary kit and suddenly began to descend into an inky abyss which blotted my vision . . .

. . . until lights bathed me as I dropped six feet to the roof of the hotel. Ouch.

Painfully standing up, I saw a silvery egg surrounding the building. The inner side of the defensive field. Nearby, the rest of the gang was gathered around Tina, who was using a pen to scratch the tar rooftop in front of a stout metal door.

Hey! A weapon got through?

It's a Bic.

Close enough for government work.

Actually, she's making a pentagram.

Natch.

There didn't seem to be anything blocking the door, but I had a sick feeling in my bowels, and the back of my teeth ached. That could only mean a single thing.

"A Death Barrier?" I guessed, kneeling beside my friends.

Busy sketching, Blanco grunted yes. "Bad one. I can get cancel, but will take while." And without further preamble she began mumbling and gesturing at the doorway.

As we waited, I gave a shiver remembering what a Death Barrier could do. Several years ago, while in Haiti dealing with some voodoo spies, a witch doctor had imprisoned us inside the foul thing. While our old mage Richard Anderson and Raul frantically composed a counterspell, I had witnessed a squirrel run by. The moment the animal crossed the barrier it had ceased to live, but the momentum of its dash kept the body moving. First the fur vanished, then skin, muscle, internal organs, bones, and finally a tiny squirrel ghost screamed in unnamable agony as it faded away.

When the wizards finally broke the magical trap, none dared question why I shot the witch doctor using fifty-seven bullets, set fire to the corpse, dynamited his juju hut and relieved myself upon his car.

Why did I use fifty-seven bullets? That was all the ammo I had.

Stopping the protective litany, the Russian gripped the empty blackness and pulled her hands apart, straining with the effort. At first, nothing seemed to happen, then the air miraculously cleared and the wizard started crawling forward.

"Move quickly," she ordered. "This last only a few seconds."

In close order, the team scurried across that all-destroying boundary. Safe on the other side, I turned to spit at the foul barrier. The globule of saliva vanished in a crackling display of sparks.

Past the Death Barrier, I could see that this was not a regulation hotel door securing the roof. Composed of a hundred different pieces of metal, interhinged like a jigsaw puzzle, the bits were held together with steel bands, closed by a ceramic disk bearing the impression of the moon with silver daggers stabbed through it. The mark of the Scion. Just looking at the disk made my eyes hurt.

"Can't get in this way," stated Tina flatly. "Soul seal. It would take more magic than a dozen mages to nullify this."

"Damnation," snarled Father Donaher in frustration, and he slammed his fist against the seal. Under the herculean blow, the porcelain disk crumbled into dust and sprinkled to the floor. The steel bands disengaged and swung away with a creak.

We shared a grin. Can't argue with success.

I borrowed a hairpin from one of the ladies, picked the lock on the real door, and we entered. What we should have seen was a dingy stairwell leading to a service elevator.

What we did see was a small swatch of floor that ended in ragged tiles over an endless vista of swirling clouds that stretched into forever. Dotting the mist were a million pieces of aerial debris and huge floating chunks of masonry. The individual floors of the hotel. Some were dripping with jungle growth. Others were trapped in a swirling hurricane. Some danced with fire, two were upside down, another was cocooned and I think one was inverted, but it was hard to tell with hotel rooms.

Gulp. Well, now we know why the Scion had brought along the whole hotel. It wasn't an armored attack fortress. They most likely just couldn't find the person with the rock! This was going to be much more difficult than originally expected.

Worse, sent Jess.

"Incoming!" cried George, and we crouched low.

Scuttling forward was a werewolf astride a winged tarantula. He held a red wizard's staff in one hand, but the other was extended as if in greeting.

"*Die!*" he screamed as a greeting, and sent a Lightning Bolt at us.

Whew. Even Dale Carnegie would shoot this guy.

Palms outward, Tina deflected the bolt with a mystical shield. Then she raced off the ledge mouthing words of power. Trapped on the ledge with no distance weapons, we were unable to do anything but watch.

Plowing straight in, Tina made a fast series of finger movements, and a dazzling beam lanced out at the enemy mage. But at the last moment, a swirling pattern of energy appeared about the man to deflect the ray. It struck a floating marble pillar, vaporizing a chunk of stone.

"Goodbye, child," sneered the fellow, and the fight began in earnest.

Fireballs and laser beams were tried at first, but such simple tricks were soon discarded. Transformations were stopped by reality checks. A Shrinking spell was countered by a Growth incantation. A Death Barrier hummed into existence and was nullified by a Jump Start. The air itself about the gesturing mages crackled with the discharge of mystical energy.

It was a battle royale between the mages. Sans her staff and spell book, Tina was at a serious disadvantage. Only her massive reserves of magic gave her any hope. Supremely confident, the werewolf was in his home, with friends on the way.

Above the mages, translucent figures of their astral forms wrestled for supremacy. Scintillating daggers of light constantly thrust and jabbed, searching for any opening large enough to reach the all-too-mortal bodies of the antagonists. Fire and water elementals danced about the wizards, roaring into gouts of steam when they touched. Flesh-eating plants erupted through the stonework of the ledge. We backed onto the roof. Spectral lawn mowers cut them down in a spray of green. We advanced to the ledge. The clouds rained thousands of scorpions, which instantly curled up and died as poisonous yellow gas fogged the sky.

Wearing NASA jetpacks, a squad of armed werewolves rose into view, went stiff and dropped dead. So much for hecklers.

Getting tough, Blanco switched tactics. Maintaining a shimmering shield with her left hand, the Russian leveled her right arm, and a massive power beam erupted from her fingers. Hungrily, the Disintegrate conjure tried to consume the red staff of the enemy mage, to burn, boil or bore its way in. But her foe grabbed the Seal of the Scion about his neck and the staff stiffly resisted. A stream of vitriolic gold splashed against the immaterial barrier of shimmering blue.

The entire hotel shuddered under the iridescent by-products of irresistable force meeting immovable object in a dazzling pyrotechnic display.

I glanced at my bare wrist.

Staring at the opponent mage, Jessica made a fist about her amulet, but nothing happened. The psi shield was stronger than ever inside their headquarters.

"We have to leave before more defenders arrive," I ordered. "If Tina wins, she'll rejoin us. If not, then we don't want to be anywhere near Bug Boy unprotected. And we still have a rescue to accomplish."

Grumpy faces. It made tactical sense, but was damn unsettling. Desert a comrade in a fight. Was the world worth this? Well, maybe Chicago, at least. Defeat would mean the end of decent pizza.

I reached for my sunglasses and cursed. Donaher was using a pair of folding binoculars to scan the different hovering floors. With only naked vision, I couldn't see anything which resembled a convention hall.

"Well?" I asked, and he shrugged.

Explosions, sword clangs and blinding coronas of energy came from the mages. The tarantula was dead, but Tina was dripping in sweat and the haughty werewolf mage seemed amused.

Touching her forehead, Jessica hesitated and then pointed towards the floor covered with jungle. It would be.

"Routine four," I declared. Separate and converge was our only hope. Maybe a few of us would get through to reach the floor and find the moonrock. I only hoped it was the correct one.

Father Donaher said a quick prayer before we activated our Fly bracelets and took off, leaving our pal to fight alone.

Tick . . . tick . . .

17

Human missiles, we streaked through the sky.

As the battle wizards disappeared behind us, we separated and took diverging routes towards Jungleland. From this new perspective, it was easy to discern that the other hotel sections were orbiting the tropical rain forest.

Several machine guns chatted at me from a chunk of building covered with ice and snow. Already at max speed, I did a few Immelmanns and banked away to befuddle their aim. Then a rocket whooshed by me. Yipes! Whether it was a LAW, Armburst or HAFLA, I had no idea. Trouble comes in many shapes. But it was definitely not a Rapier or Amsterdam, because I lived to tell the tale.

Another rocket. And then an arbalist arrow.

More machine-gun fire. This time with tracer bullets. Fast, I did a Hammerstall to build speed and barreled straight in towards my goal. Speed was my best defense now.

The target floor loomed before me, rapidly increasing in size. A full tropical jungle overflowed the hotel piece, vines and creepers hanging over the edge. Just floating in the air like that, it resembled an Amazonian plateau, without the plat.

Coming closer, the greenery became individual trees, the growth cleared into bushes with leaves and I crashed in going head over heels. Roll, Alvarez, roll! It'll help cushion the impact. Didn't help when you hit a tree, though. Ow!

Extricating myself from the brambles, I found my bottle of Healing potion and took a swig. The pain diminished. Ah. Now, where was the gang?

Over here! Ten meters towards the volcano.

What? Oh, there it was. Wow.

Hurrying, I found them in a small clearing of bare ground,

with a matching set of chairs and sofa surrounded by lush vegetation.

Renault had a long stick that he was frantically trying to sharpen a point on with a jagged rock. Donaher was tying his ceremonial purple sash around three stones to fashion a crude bolero. Jessica was plucking leaves off a vine already knotted into a garrote. Way to go, Tunafish! We were down but not out.

Removing my shoes, I knelt and filled a sock with dirt. Called a tap, cosh, persuader, blackjack, sap, whatever, it was one of the oldest weapons created by humans, but it was still here because it worked so well. Totally silent and reusable, a sap hit like a sledgehammer and could kill in trained hands. Mine.

I tested a swing on a palm. My flesh stung from the mild impact. Cracking open its skull and pulverizing the brain should slow down even the strongest werewolf. I hoped.

"Okay, standard search pattern," I said. "But this time we stay together. Double coverage. Me and Jess, George and Mike."

"Hold," whispered Jessica. "There's something out there."

We moved into a defensive posture. Straining vision, I could dimly perceive a misshapen thing moving through the jungle circling our position. We could clearly hear the steady tap of multiple feet.

"What is it?" queried George, peering against the darkness of the trees.

"Another tarantula?" guessed Father Donaher, starting to swing his bolero. The stones clicked once, and soft as the noise was, the creature instantly scuttled forward in our direction.

"Manticore!" hissed Jessica as the monster burst from the foliage.

The silver-blue illumination from the magical sky highlighted its bloated hairy body. Ugly bugger. Part spider, part scorpion, and part cockroach, the very name of the demonic insect meant death in several dimensions.

George heaved his makeshift spear and missed. Mike

threw the bolero and hit, with no effect. Before the rest of us could move, a stream of brackish liquid squirted from the mouth of the insect to hit Renault in the face. With a hideous gargle, the man fell, clawing at his smoking flesh.

The manticore vomited a second stream of death at me. I ducked and Donaher leapt upon the back of the beast and buried his cross in the mottled hump like a dagger. Poison blood squirted across the glowing crucifix and ignited. Mike dove for the bushes. In a juicy crackle, the mutant bug burst into flames. Bleeding fire, it charged into the bushes. A moment later we heard its death scream fading into the distance. Downward.

We sprinted to Renault.

Biting his tongue not to scream, George clawed feebly for his canteen. Pushing the hands aside, I poured a full bottle of Healing potion on the soldier's face. There was a violent hiss and he relaxed. As the fumes dispersed and his countenance became visible, we tried not to gasp in horror.

George's face was a ghastly greenish yellow, the flesh puckered into ravines of gnarled skin. But even worse, his eyes were featureless orbs of solid white.

"Will . . . will I live?" he croaked.

I gave it to him straight. "Yes. But you're blind."

He took the bitter news stolidly.

"Healing potion?"

"Tried already."

Gingerly, the man fingered his face.

"How bad is it?" George asked in a small voice.

"Oh, I've seen worse."

"Never play poker with me, Ed. That terrible, eh?"

I told him yes.

Gamely, he stood. "Come on, we still got a world to save."

With Donaher on guard, Jessica was already busy. Holding a forked branch by the ends, she walked around in circles searching for a secret door, hidden entrance. Maybe even the elevator. That would be nice.

Fat chance, bucko. She stopped. "We dig here."

Using our hands, we scooped aside the loose soil until we

reached concrete. Guided into place, Renault slammed the steel-reinforced heel of his army boots onto the material and after a few tries it started to crack. Pieces came loose, and bending low, we pried them aside.

Below was a hotel corridor.

"I'm staying here," said Renault, crawling to the nearby bushes and pulling branches loose. "I'll cover the hole and try to sidetrack any werewolves."

Blind with a stick. I would add the name of Renault to the heroes roll of Horatio and Audie Murphy.

Mike and I shook his hands, Jess gave him a hug and we dropped down inside.

We found ourselves near a curtained window at the end of a hallway lined with doors. The carpet was decorated with party favors and every door had a dining tray loaded with plates and liquor bottles. Women's underwear hung from the doorknobs. These occult conventions must be pretty wild.

There were no numbers; each door had a brass plate and was named after a President. Yep, this was the convention floor. I tried a knob and found it unlocked. Peeking inside, I saw the ocean. Donaher cracked a door and confronted a desert plain. Jess peered at the Alps. A goat wandered by.

We closed the doors. How many dimensions and places was this poor befuddled building occupying at the same instant?

Tick . . . tick . . .

As the doors would lead us nowhere, in triangle formation we skirted forward in the corridor, ready for attack. This deep in the enemy's citadel, anything could happen.

Turning a corner, we encountered an elderly woman with white hair and a cane.

"You!" cried the oldster and Jess.

My wife grabbed the amulet around her neck as the elderly woman extended a fist adorned with a huge signet ring. Motionless, they stood there locked in silent battle. It was only specks at first, then glowing sparks started swirling about the two telepaths, and soon they were encased in a vortex of static discharges from the awful load of mental energies unleashed.

Donaher started to reach for them and I stopped him.

"Don't," I warned the priest. "It'd kill you."

Frowning, Mike touched the empty shotgun holster on his belt.

"Come on," I said, and forced myself to take that first step away from my wife.

That's when the reinforcements arrived. Two of them, in flak jackets and carrying M-16 machine guns.

Moving fast, we stepped close to the monsters. Now standing behind the muzzle, the guns could no longer harm us. It was apparently a trick the Scion agents had never heard of, as their jaws unhinged. In grim satisfaction, I swung my cosh and Mike smacked the other in the face with his armored Bible. Bones crunched in stereo.

Reeling backwards, the wolves stumbled to the floor. We pounded them again for a while until they stopped moving. Quickly, we stripped them of flak jackets, pistols and ammo clips. They even had one grenade apiece. How nice! Old WWII-style pineapples loaded with blasting powder and gelignite, but serviceable nonetheless.

Sprawled on the carpet, the werewolves were already starting to moan back into life. It takes more than a simple beating to kill a were. No problem. Bureau 13 agents are most obliging.

Dragging the bodies around a corner, we jammed them into a closet. The Donaher and I each stuffed our sole grenade into the mouth of the respective victim, pulled the pins, slammed the door and ran. Thunder and flame filled the hallway in our wake, but we kept going. Let's see how quickly they heal with no heads.

As we raced along the corridors, I checked the load on a clip. U.S.Army-issue regulation 5.56mm perfectly imbalanced tumblers. Nasty bullets that enter a shoulder, ricochet around, chewing the major organs to mincemeat, and then exit from the opposite hip. I had been hoping for phosphorous tracer rounds or mercury-tipped explosive bullets. Might as well wish for the blessed silver. Still they were something.

At the elevator bank, a sign on an easel announced the

times and locations of numerous convention functions. There was no listing for the moonrock.

With a musical ding the central elevator doors parted to display a score of werewolves with fire axes and pistols.

"Pinocchio!" I screamed, aiming the M-16 at the wall above the cage. Donaher added the firepower of his M-16 and we spent an entire clip chewing a hole in the wall.

Crack!

After the initial shock of seeing us, and the gunfight with nobody, the grinning and drooling werewolves started towards us. With a sharp twang, the weakened elevator cable snapped and down they went.

"Safety brakes will stop them from crashing, in only a few stories," grumped Mike, peering after them.

"There aren't any more stories," I reminded him.

Suddenly, light bathed his face as the cage left the shaft. Distant screaming. "Well, at least they're out of the way."

"Yeah."

As the doors automatically closed, we returned to business.

"NASA doesn't allow you to charge admission to see the rock," said the priest, "so it must be in the main public area."

"But immediately near your ticket booth to entice folks inside to see more marvels," I added.

"Main conference room?"

I agreed. There was a map of the floor on the wall. We smashed the glass and peeled it off the frame. Hmm, big hotel.

His finger stabbed at the map. "There it is. Down this corridor, make a left, three doors, right."

I rolled the floor plan and tucked it into my belt.

"Let's go."

18

We had only taken a step when Mike gasped in pain. I turned about and saw him taking his hand away from his right hip. The palm was covered with red.

"They shot me," he said, surprised.

The big priest started wobbling a bit and I slid a chair underneath him. Under the cassock, his pants and shirt were dripping with blood. Tenderly, I probed the wound.

He inhaled sharply. "It's in my hip."

"Can't get a tourniquet there," I stated. Feeling in my pockets, I found the bottle of Healing potion. Empty.

"Mine's also gone," groaned Father Donaher. He was a bit pale by now and starting to sweat. That was the way most small-caliber bullet wounds worked. At first your body rejected the pain, but with blood loss it was soon undeniable. I touched his throat, searching for the carotid artery. His pulse was up, yet his temperature was down. Sweaty and clammy. There was major internal hemorrhaging. He was dying.

"Wanna do a George?" I asked, feeling a lump in my throat.

He exhaled mightily and nodded yes.

I ripped off my white shirt and folded it into a compress, using my tie to hold it in place. The belt would have worked better but I needed that to keep up my pants.

With Donaher's weakening assistance, I moved the chair to the wall and dragged a sofa in front. There: back protected and some cover to hide behind. Good enough.

Dripping sweat, Mike gave me a shaky thumbs-up and I hurriedly departed. It was my job now. Alone.

Rounding a corner, I bumped into somebody holding a Wichita Thunderbolt pistol. I aimed and fired the M-16 in the same move.

Annoyed, J. P. Withers looked down the line of puckered bullet holes in his chest.

"If you didn't want my help," he growled, "you only had to say so. No need to be rude." And Withers vanished.

"No, wait!" I cried to the empty corridor. Damn the man!

The I paused. Wait a minute, if he Gated in, then were the runes down? Was help on the way? There was no way to know. I hurried onward.

At a pair of double doors with tiny decorative windows set in them, I stayed low and peeked through. Exhibit Hall A.

Surrounding a ticket booth, sparkling layers of nonreality swirled and spun in a multicolored light show of dimensional instability. Countless phantasms strolled along, crossing from one world to the next; transparent fish swam by, ghostly flocks of birds, spectral racing cars, an ethereal cavalry charge, a spirited elephant stampede. The floor bucked and writhed like a living thing. The walls pulsed and the ceiling constantly broke apart, the acoustic tiles sliding over each other to endlessly rearrange themselves.

On the ground were the charred bones of the Marine honor guard that accompanied the moonrock wherever it went. Behind the velvet ropes was a little old lady poised in the act of lifting the unearthly object from the Lucite base. Bingo!

And something hit me from behind. Burning pain filled my skull and I felt my heart slow . . . down . . . and . . . st . . .

. . . art again! Completely healed, I sat upright and blew smoke out of my mouth. The copper bracelet on my wrist gave one last tingle and went still. Whew. Whoever had killed me left too soon. That was the third and last Jump Start I had ever experienced. My quota was filled. I could never again use the death-or-life emergency Healing spell.

Once more, I peeked into the main exhibit hall. Stalking around on patrol was a werewolf holding a crimson-splattered fire axe. That was my blood and brains on the blade! Boy, was I pissed off now! In a curse that was more snarl than words, I kicked open the doors and cut loose with the M-16.

"Eat silver, bozo!" I screamed.

The stuttering stream of army tumblers stitched the monster's torso, shoving him backwards until it hit the marble wall and collapsed to the floor, twisted and bleeding.

". . . should have known . . . silver bullets," coughed the monster weakly.

Trying my best to radiate confidence, I moved towards the lady and rock. I was almost there when the werewolf clawed at his chest, pulling one of the slugs free with a faint sucking sound. He stared at the grayish lump.

"Just a darn minute," growled the beast, the flow of blood from its wounds slowing. "This isn't silver!"

"Sue me!" I sneered, hosing another full clip into the monster.

As the air cleared, I could see that the creature had literally been cut in half by the fusillade. Howling in agony, the werewolf was writhing about on the floor, his claws digging sharp furrows into the crimson-splattered stone. Ha!

Then I watched horrified as the Scion werewolf pulled on its legs as a man would don pants. Whole once more, the beast stood and hobbled forward in a weak charge.

I glanced at a huge clock placed prominently on the wall. One hand was spinning backwards, while the other hung limp. Swell.

"Gonna . . . eat . . . then kill . . . you," snarled the man-beast.

Slamming in the last clip, I didn't bother to reply. The heavy-combat rounds made the creature jerk with every impact, but nothing more.

Out of bullets, I hurled the rifle and hopped over the velvet ropes. There was still a chance to rescue the lady. I had a teleport bracelet. If I used it on her instead of me . . .

Something got my collar and I was yanked backwards to hit the floor. As claws reached for my face, I delivered a killing karate chop to the kidney. I was no Mindy Jennings, but I had been trained by her.

As the werewolf howled in pain, I rolled to my feet, and spinning about, kicked his knee, feeling the bone crunch under the edge of my shoe. The beast staggered and almost fell. Then he stood, whole and undamaged, and rising to his full eight feet in height, roared like the primordial beast he was!

"Your momma," I growled, and kicked him in the groin.

Gasping in pain, the werewolf raked its claws at me. Gracefully, I bowed beneath the blow, stepped in and rammed both of my fists into the jaw of the creature with trip-hammer force.

Bruised, the werewolf shook off the tap and butted me hard. I saw the ceiling go by as I went flying to smack against the wall with a sickening crack. Disoriented, I staggered to my feet. Bemused, the unshaven Scion agent laughed, a mistake that nearly cost him a jaw. Shouting a martial arts battle cry, I leapt and hit the man-beast in a flying kick, powered by my full hundred and fifty pounds of Wyoming ranch muscle. Kill me, will you?

Stunned, the werewolf staggered, so I pressed the attack home. Had to get this yutz off me so I could 'port the old lady out of here. How close were we to O'Hare? How soon till the missiles blew us all to Hell? My sunfist broke the nose of the monster, cupped hands slapped against its pointed ears, rupturing eardrums. A finger jab nearly removed an eye. I was concentrating on the werewolf's head, probably the only vulnerable spot the creature had. If any.

No longer amused by this game, the enraged werewolf thrust his paws downward to rend me apart. I barely managed to sway out of the way, the front of my body armor ripping free, three red lines on my stomach oozing blood. Oh crap! This close to the epicenter of the ethereal vortex, the protective spell on my T-shirt had been nullified! Again, I ducked under a fist the size of an express train. Dive-rolling past the hairy titan, I tripped on the ropes as a foot slammed on the floor, cracking the marble. Since it was so close, I did the only logical act and buried my teeth into the shin of the monster. Hey, any damage done to an opponent, no matter how minor, was a point in your favor. Crunching hard, my mouth filled with the coppery taste of blood. Bleh.

Frantically, the werewolf shook me off. Scrambling to my feet, I grabbed a hairy arm and tossed the giant creature over my shoulder in a classic judo throw. The monster hit the floor like a sack of wet newspapers advertising cement.

Groggily, the creature struggled erect and faced me eye-to-eye. Eh? When had the beast shrunk?

Suddenly shrieking, the werewolf seemed to blur as ripples of change spread outward from the trivial wound in its leg. Hair follicles withdrew into the skin, its jaw shortened, fangs shrank and ears became round and pink.

Catching my breath, I had a flash of understanding. According to the legends, if a person was bitten by a werewolf, he became a werewolf. So, maybe to cure a werewolf, what you had to do was—bite him? Well, waddayano.

In stark terror, the transforming monster tried to escape, but I tripped him. Scrunching his face, the Scion agent tried to countermand the transformation. But it proved unstoppable, and soon I was towering over a naked man with the most amazingly innocent expression on his face.

"Why, I am cured!" he cried joyously. "It is like I have awakened from a bad dream."

Oh brother, now tell me the one about the magic bunny. I guess my face showed my feelings, because he went pale.

"Don't you believe me, Officer?" asked the runt, a sickly grin on his face.

Now, how would he know I was a cop unless he remembered his actions as a werewolf?

"Should have copped the Fifth, pal," I told him, and hit the killer with every ounce of strength I possessed.

The blow nearly succeeded in melding nose to ear. Spinning like a drugged top, the scrawny killer spewed blood and teeth as he toppled to the floor, nowhere near as dead as he deserved.

Turning, I kicked over the ropes and advanced for the rock lady. But then from the midst of the raging dimensional storm came a dark flash, followed by a sucking retort. Everything went calm. And with a sick feeling in my stomach, I knew the Fly spell had just been canceled.

The hotel was starting to fall.

Retreating a meter, I charged at the old woman. Instantly, I was bombarded by delusionary madness: scenes from my

personal past, movie clips, TV commercials and vignettes
from the legitimate theatre. Her eyes watched me, frozen in
her own horror. Struggling to retain my sanity, I fought my
way through the phantasmal hordes of historical figures and
cartoon caricatures. Step by step, I advanced, grimly determined to reach her or die. My heart began to pound wildly.
My skin tightened painfully, my bones shifted positions, my
hair began to grow . . . *Jumping Jesus, I was becoming a
werewolf!*

As ghostly bicycles raced through the room, I threw myself forward against the hurricane force of the space-twisting
rift. Stretching until I thought joints would pop, I just barely
managed to slip the bracelet on her skinny wrist.

Home! I mentally screamed. *HOMEHOMEHOME!*

And she vanished. Taking the transdimensional vortex
with her.

Still braced to counter the ethereal winds, I was caught off
balance and hit the floor. Success! Chicago was safe! Ouch.

My joy dimmed as giant cracks appeared in the floor, and
the ticket booth collapsed. The whole damn hotel was shuddering from the raw velocity of its unchecked plummet. I always knew this job would kill me someday. Well, at least it
would be quick.

No. Wait a minute, I'm in a hotel for an occult convention!

Adrenaline rushing in my veins, I glanced about. With the
departure of the moonrock, now exposed on the other side of
the exhibit hall was a line of dealer's booths. Struggling to
keep my balance on the disco-dancing floor, I did a fast inventory of the magical paraphernalia: crystal balls, books,
pyramids, Tarot cards, Ouija boards, cassette tapes, knives,
rugs. Rugs! Yes! But my sunglasses were long gone. How
was I supposed to know which was real and which the sham?

Gathering air into my lungs, I shouted a Word of Power
above the deafening noise of cracking concrete. A rug at the
bottom of the pile seemed to tremble. Maybe it was just my
imagination. Then again, maybe not. I yanked it free, sending the rest of the carpets tumbling to the floor.

The doorway collapsed and the windows exploded. Icy

winds howled throughout the hotel, tearing the fixtures off the walls.

Rummaging in the debris, I found an assortment of ornamental daggers. Hoped they were clean. Snatching a serpentine kiris, I sliced my palm and squeezed a fist, letting the drops fall onto the carpet.

"One is for thy weaver." Drip. "One is for thy master." Drip. Oh hell, what was next? Ah, yes. "One is for thee." Drip. "And three is for me." Drip, drip, drip.

Nothing happened.

As the building started to break apart around me, I angrily drop-kicked the carpet. "Fly, damn you!"

Instantly, the woven cloth went rigid, hovering at knee level. *Banzai!* Grabbing another carpet, I hopped onto the Egyptian Express, wrapping a second rug tight around me. God, I hoped this worked.

The curtains and carpet burst into flames, and a steel I-beam pierced a wall coming dangerously close.

"Get me out of here!"

Wafting casually, it headed for the stairs.

"Straight through the window!" I screamed. "And don't spare the horsehairs!"

There was motion. Glass exploded and I was in the starry black sky. Yowsa! When this thing cut loose, even Renault would be impressed with the speed. I decided to name it Runner.

Shucking my protective wrap, I watched the building fall. Sadly, I observed that the individual pieces had joined together and it was a completely whole ten-story building hurtling down towards . . . hey, that wasn't O'Hare! Or Chicago!

No, it isn't.

Jess!

Who else?

No coherent thoughts came to mind.

How sweet. I love you also. And to bring you up to date on current events, using his and Tina's wands, Raul Gated the whole damn building away from any populated area.

Brilliant! Where?

She told me, and with a contented smile, I settled in to watch the show. From this high upward, I should have a splendid view of the crash.

A trail of flame stretched out behind the rocketing hotel like a comet's tail. Knifing through the cloud layer, the hotel reached and went past Mach 1. With a sonic boom, the building broke apart again, the chunks continuing like a shotgun blast.

What remained of the hotel crashed precisely in the middle of Hadleyville, West Virginia, instantly converting into 700 million ergs of pure radiant heat.

In a blinding flash, the stores and homes disappeared, everything pulverized by the sheer force of the concussion. Jagged cracks spread out from the impact point like earthly lightning bolts. Motionless for a million geological years, the nearby Appalachian Mountains danced from the shock waves, but contained the brunt of the nuclear-grade explosion.

Clutching the fringe of Runner, I held on for dear life and rode the volcanic storming as best I could.

After what seemed to be an eternity, the rumbling vibrations ceased and an eerie stillness enshrouded the decimated headquarters of the Scion with a graveyard peace.

Ha!

Epilogue

We never heard from the Scion of the Silver Dagger again.

After Tina beat her mage, and Jess killed her evil counterpart, they rushed to join the fight, rescuing George and saving the good father's life. Mike walks with a wooden cane these days. A cane from Remington Industries that fires 12 gauge shotgun shells, of course.

Our jetsam equipment crashed in farmland and the only victims were an assortment of young squash. How appropriate.

A short phone call from Horace Gordon, and NASA started replacing their moonrocks on display with precise duplicates tooled from rocks from Ganymede, a moon of Jupiter. Who's going to know the difference? It cost them a pretty penny, but after that "special favor" we did for them, it was considered only fair payment.

Our Cyber-Cops had wisely fled the vicinity of Hadleyville when the sky began falling and we didn't lose a single robot.

In less than a month, Mathais Bolt and most of the top echelon of the Brotherhood of Darkness were arrested for committing a wide variety of crimes directly traceable to them by the money I had marked inside that safe. Snicker.

The crew of the U.S.S. *Idaho* was rescued, and with the assistance of the Bureau mermaids, we even managed to save the mighty battleship herself. The mass marriage is next month. Oh, those crazy sailors.

It took microsurgeons from West Virginia to remove the moonrock from the fist of Dr. Joanne Abernathy, but she has a nice robotic replacement and doesn't really mind. And after a pep talk from Horace Gordon, it appears that Dr.

Abernathy will be joining our august organization. Lord knows we can always use trained medical personnel.

Our running battle on the Ohio Turnpike was declared a shoot-out between rival drug gangs. The firefights in Chicago attributed to mob warfare. The *Idaho* officially never sank.

Surreptitiously exposed to the truth about the supernatural threats to America, the Bureau received over a thousand recruits from every branch of the Justice Department and Department of Defense. For the first time since the slaughter of '77 we have a full complement of agents.

Enough agents for me to propose a very special mission that was flatly refused by the Bureau as too damn dangerous. However, I did have some vacation time coming my way . . .

Runner and Amigo have become the best of friends. If only we could stop them from taking joyrides and strafing the zoo. The dry-cleaning bills are killing us!

Damaged from her deadly psionic battle, Jessica found that her telepathic powers had been reduced to her natural level. Me is visiting a psychologist and getting some treatment for its manic depression.

We got a new RV.

After rebuilding the downtown Chicago apartment building, we sold it on the open market. My team was becoming too well known in Chicago, so we switched locations with another team and started the laborious process of altering a warehouse in an industrial park of Columbus, Ohio. No more tenants!

An old dead friend of ours, Abduhl Benny Hassan, moved into the basement of the new building. This pleased everybody, especially Mindy. Without a ghost in the basement, it just wasn't home.

Besides, Abdul has no objection to materializing back to Chicago once a week and getting us a real pizza from Carmen's on Sheridan Avenue. Still hot when it arrives too. Flat pizza? Bleh.

Meanwhile, Mr. Renault is in the Geneva Medical Institute recovering from the latest rounds of plastic surgery. He'll be fine. And resembling a short Sean Connery if the lovely Ms. Blanco has anything to say about his facial reconstruction.

Bureau 13 headquarters is no longer located in the Sears Tower.

The Lazy Eight Motel was renamed the Fab Four Motel.

I started growing hair every full moon, but with monthly anti-lycanthropy shots and a sharp razor I'm doing fine.

The fight between the buxom ThunderBunnies and the Colombian mercenaries at the Museum of Science and Industry will be released next summer by TriStar Pictures. Rated H. No heart attack patients or heretics allowed.

To this day, J. P. Withers will not talk to me.

The task required the Army Corps of Engineers to divert a West Virginia river, but they managed to flood the impact crater from the hotel, and a private investment company started construction on Meteor Lake Amusement Park. And we helped design the Haunted House. It's the best part-time job I ever had. See you there.

Boo.